NIGHTMARES

AT YE

OLDE ELM TREE

BARRY HILLIER

Barry Hillier

Copyright © 2020

BARRY HILLIER

<u>Fictional content</u>

A majority of the book

FOREWARD

I was once a proud owner of a busy village public house and restaurant, in the heart of Wiltshire. A welcoming, classic old English country pub, with its thatched roof, stone walls, inglenook fireplaces, good food, quality ales and wines.

It was a similar age to **Ye Olde Elm Tree**, the public house that I have created for this paranormal story. There were some strange, unexplainable happenings that took place in our old pub. There were a few locals, with some chilling stories too. I have used a few of our experiences, in this book.

Just before we sold the business on, we were visited by a group of 'ghost hunters.' They found nine 'hot spots' throughout the building. For each location there was a story to tell. I understand that an exorcism has since taken place there.

I once said to my daughter Kirstie, that I had thought of an enthralling start, to a supernatural fiction story. I had also thought of a captivating end to the tale as well. It was March 2020, the Coronavirus was sweeping the world, it was lockdown in Britain. 'Now would be a good time to start your book Dad' suggested Kirstie. So, I created chapter one and emailed it to Kirstie and our son-in-law Gary, their feedback and enthusiasm was extremely valuable, so chapter two was born, and so was my book

'Nightmares at Ye Olde Elm Tree.'

Barry Hillier

ACKNOWLEDGEMENTS

I must thank my lovely wife Sue. For the fifteen weeks we were in lockdown together, we had some great walks every day, we are lucky to live in a picturesque corner of Wiltshire. Most evenings, Sue would encourage me to spend time on my book. While I was tapping away on my PC keyboard, Sue would demonstrate her skills, by preparing some delicious meals. When a chapter was finished, I would often read it to Sue, her love and inspiration for my project, was motivational.

Back in 2007, I produced a murder mystery game, that was not published at the time. So, I do hope you enjoy my first book, by taking this investigative, supernatural journey with me.

I would sincerely like to thank friends, Mike Thompson, Jo and Julian Harvey, and Caroline Henham, for helping to sanity check elements of this book.

Thank you, to Claire Walton for her imaginative and artistic design of the book cover.

I must thank too, author Joy Wodhams, who has a dozen books to her collection, with several more intriguing novels to follow. Her warm and friendly advice on publishing a fiction novel, was really appreciated.

My daughter Kirstie and son-in-law Gary, were both working throughout the lockdown, in essential services and the NHS. Juggling busy work schedules, whilst teaching and entertaining two young daughters, Ella and Isabel at home. So, I would like to say a huge thank you to Kirstie and Gary; for in the evenings, they still found the time to read each chapter of this book, as it arrived, hot off the press.

CHAPTER 1 – JOURNEY'S END

Steve Aylott was a dashing, debonair, sales manager. Thirty-nine, wavy dark hair, a rugby physique, he kissed his wife Julie goodbye on their front doorstep. Walking out to his Mercedes parked on the front drive, carrying a suit carrier over his shoulder he called out to Julie,

'See you late Friday, have fun with the kids this week.' Steve and Julie had three boys, ten, seven and five.

He drove five miles to pick up his colleague, Geoff Foreman, a sales manager much different to Steve, forty-nine, balding, on his third marriage. Geoff had a cabin bag rather than a suitor, he was wearing his suit for the journey from Dorset, to where the sales meeting was to take place, near Loch Lomond.

Steve then drove a further three miles to pick up their new sales assistant, Jack Hardwick. Twenty-three, boyish looks, Jack wore separates to travel in, a trendy check jacket and jeans. Jack lived with his parents, two sisters and a brother, in a cramped country cottage. His folks were there at the door to wish him luck. Jack had been with the company just six months and this was to be his first sales meeting, he was quite excited.

The three stopped off for a brunch at a motorway service station. 'I'll get the late breakfasts,' said Steve. 'Full English all round and coffees?'

'Yes,' was the answer except Geoff asked for a pot of tea.

Steve had planned a stop off at an overnight stay to break the journey. It was a remote public house and inn, in the Lake District, nearest village one mile, called the Ye Olde Elm Tree.

The inn, reputed to be over three hundred years old, had a simple website. Four cosy bedrooms, bar and smokers lounge, the latter had never been updated by the sole Licensee, Annie X. She never had time to have her surname inserted, the website was never finished. Vince Compton who was constructing the website, something had scared him, he never returned to finish it.

Geoff had been awarded top salesman at Trinder for the last six consecutive years. Since Steve had joined the company two years ago, there was clearly more competition for the top spot. They liked to act as big chums to their peers but there was an underlying striving, to gain sales, amongst the two of them.

The long journey covered a multitude of conversations, some work related, business competition, customers, sales tactics. Jack eagerly listening to the conversations from the back seat, sometimes leaning forward to catch every word. Family discussions, social chat, holidays. On places where Geoff and Steve had holidayed, that conversation was quite competitive!

As they approached the Lake District the weather had started to really deteriorate. The motorway section of the journey, as they ventured further north, had several delays due to heavy rain. It was late afternoon, dark, dismal, almost dusk.

'Where the hell are you taking us Steve?' asked Geoff in a sarcastic manor.

'Well the Sat-Nav says only another half an hour and we'll reach the pub,' said Steve. 'We can grab a few beers, grab something to eat and cosy down for the evening.'

'Is there far to travel in the morning?' asked Jack.

'No,' replied Steve, 'Couple of hours, we can get an early start and grab breakfast on route, like today.'

As the conversation finished, Steve's Mercedes hit an unexpected large puddle on the road, which threw the car sideways. Steve did well to control the skid, as the car seemed to travel sideways for quite a distance.

'That was lucky that there was nothing coming the other way,' gasped Steve.

'Mother of God,' replied Geoff as he shook his head in disbelief.

Jack looked down on his side of the road; there was quite a drop below. As Jack reflected on what might have been, his mouth remained wide open.

After a series of double bends in the road they saw an incline ahead with some faint lights near the top of the hill.

'Reckon that could be the pub Geoff, where those lights are ahead,' said Steve.

As they climbed the hill Geoff commented on how chilly the air had become, 'If we weren't nearly there, Steve, I might get you to give us a quick blast with the car heater,' said Geoff as he rubbed his hands together.

'Yes, it's gone very cold all of a sudden,' piped up Jack from the back of the car.

They finally reached Ye Olde Elm Tree, a dimly lit stone building; the gravel car park was adjacent to the pub surrounded by high stone walls. There was only one car in the car park, a vintage Morris Minor. Geoff thought that was a bit odd. Steve pulled up in a corner at the far end of the car park.

'Why such a walk to the pub?' asked Geoff.

'Chance to stretch our legs,' said Steve with a wry smile.

To their horror the car had started to sink into the ground. Looking puzzled Steve restarted the engine and tried to reverse from the spot where he had parked. The wheels were just spinning. Digging themselves further into the ground.

'What the hell is happening?' called out Geoff.

'No idea mate, but we look well and truly stuck,' replied Steve.

At that point, the car sunk further. All three men tried to open their car doors, but they were all jammed by the wet muddy soil and gravel. As each door opened ajar the mud came seeping into the footwells of the car.

'Close your doors everyone,' shouted Steve. 'We're letting too much mud into the car.'

Each slammed their door shut. Then the engine died. Geoff and Steve glanced at each other in total bewilderment.

'What's happening Steve?' yelled Jack as the vehicle continued to sink in the ground.

'Let's try the windows,' said Steve in a sense of panic. The car had no electrics, the windows would not open.

'I'll have to break my window,' Steve yelled.

Geoff just watched Steve in fear, hoping he could break his window and they would be able to escape this sudden nightmare. Jack tried to break his window too, with his feet. Seconds passed and the mud was now almost at window level. Then there was an almighty sound of glass cracking. Steve had managed to crack the window, then he painfully put his elbow through the glass. Pushing the remaining fragments away, he hauled himself through the window.

'This is more like quicksand than mud,' wailed Steve as he dived head-first into it.

Geoff tried to follow but by now the mud had started to pour through Steve's open window. Mud was also pouring into the car from under the dashboard.

Jack was hysterical, 'We're all going to die,' and started to try and smash his back window open once again. Jack was frantic. 'Help us, help us,' he cried in desperation.

Steve slowly disappeared into the mud his arms outstretched as the ground sucked him under. Steve was gone. It seemed only seconds later that the ground had engulfed the Mercedes, frightened yells and screams came from within the car as it sunk into the ground. There were whirlpools of slushing mud for a short while, followed by an eerie stillness and silence.

Just then at the side of the pub, high in the apex of the roof was a small dimly lit window. In it was a face of an elderly woman. It was Annie X the licensee.

CHAPTER 2 – YE OLDE ELM TREE

Annie couldn't sleep that night. She tossed and turned in her bed, she couldn't get out of her head what she saw earlier that day. Those poor men in that car. How did that possibly happen? People have parked in that spot previously. She has been living at the pub near on ten years and there has never been an incident in the car park, other than the occasional bump, mainly from alcohol. How was that corner of the car park so muddy? It was like a swamp.

She kept telling herself it didn't happen. It couldn't happen. That she imagined the whole thing. But to counteract that she thought; that's why Mr Aylott, Foreman and Hardwick didn't show up to claim their rooms they booked last night. They must have been in that car. How horrific.

Annie went downstairs at 3.30 am and made herself a cup of tea. What should she do about that corner of the car park? I'll have to fence it off somehow, she thought.

8 am Annie was on the phone to the local general handyman Bob Truman.

'Good morning Annie,' said Bob answering his mobile phone. 'You are up nice and early this morning, couldn't you sleep?'

'Bob, I need you to do an urgent job,' said Annie with an impulsive manner.

Bob sensed some anxiety in Annie's voice. 'Well I am a bit busy with a few odd jobs at the moment Annie.'

Annie interrupted him. 'You must come over now Bob there is something I need you to do as the holiday season will start up in a few weeks. Please Bob.'

'Ok Annie, look I'll be over late afternoon and see what's so urgent.' The receiver went dead on Bob, Annie had hung up.

Bob carried on getting his tools out of his van, reflecting back on his conversation with Annie. She was such a calm, harmonious character normally. Yet this morning, she seemed distressed. The last time Bob had heard her like that was on the tragic death of her husband Bert.

Bob turned up at Ye Olde Elm Tree just after 4 pm. Parked his van next to the Morris Minor. Annie came out of the front door, she looked drawn and haggard, as if she had seen a ghost.

'Ah Bob I need you to fence off the corner of the car park, near that willow tree,' said Annie. 'But whatever you do don't stand anywhere near the corner, as the ground can be very soft, sometimes swampy.' She spoke with a tremble in her voice.

Bob looked puzzled. The ground looked fine to him.

'Won't that limit your parking during holiday season Annie?' asked Bob.

'I can't afford any of my customers' cars to get stuck if the ground gets soft, when can you start Bob?' Annie asked with trepidation.

'How about at the weekend?' Bob replied.

'Fine,' said Annie 'Thanks,' and walked back into the pub.

Bob thought that was strange as Annie never even asked him for a price!

Ye Olde Elm Tree was reputed to have been built over three hundred years ago. The original occupancy was that of a farmhouse with land stretching over twenty acres. In the late 1860's the main house was used by the family as a Wesleyan Church; a holiness Methodist Christian denomination, originating from America with roots in the teachings of preacher John Wesley. This was the building's main purpose until the First World War, 1914-1918, when it was said that the owner and his two sons were all lost in the Great War. Any family that remained must have moved on, as the property became derelict for many years. It was written that many of the church's worshippers and followers were buried somewhere local, although there is no trace of any graveyard anywhere near at present.

In 1929 a local builder John Covington purchased the property and later sold off much of the adjoining farmland. His intention was always to renovate the old house as his family home with extensive gardens. He was very proud of the bar he built in his main sitting room. In the 1930's John started brewing beer, which became very popular with the local community.

Sadly, John met a tragic death. He was found in his garden part submerged into the ground, as if he were unable to move, which led him to have a cardiac arrest. His beer reputation however lived on as Benjamin Hoskins, a local brewer, bought the property and turned it into a public house. It was first called the King's Arms as Benjamin Hoskins was renowned to be a staunch royalist.

Nightmares at Ye Olde Elm Tree

There were many owners of the King's Arms in the years that followed. It was a conversation piece with many of the locals, how several owners had met tragic deaths, lots of rumours. When Albert (Bert) and Annie Baines bought the property lease ten years previously, Bert decided to rename the Pub. He didn't much like the King's Arms and he was personally drawn to the old elm tree at the bottom of the garden. Bert would often eat his lunch laid up against the tree on a nice sunny day. Although he often told Annie he often thought he could hear voices down there! Because of the age of the building he decided to call it Ye Olde Elm Tree.

It was a Tuesday evening, Annie played host to a card school for a group of locals. Their favourite games were chase the lady, auction bridge and cribbage. Just six in the bar that night. Local farmer Geoffrey Forde, a dairy farmer, liked to sit at the end of the bar, enjoy a couple of pints and read the newspaper. That was how he would unwind after a busy day. Annie always supplied the paper for Farmer Forde. He would jump in his pickup truck afterwards, eat a big dinner, early to bed to attend to those cows in the morning.

Monica was a widow. Her husband was Bert & Annie's gardener at the pub. It was a terrible tragedy, when his body was pulled out of the pub's fishpond a few years previously. There was no apparent explanation on what had happened. Monica became quite a close friend to Annie especially after Landlord Bert's tragic death. Monica's tipple was a gin and tonic, she would chat to Annie most of the evening, Farmer Forde would occasionally join in but only if it suited him.

13

In the card school was retired fireman Julian (Jules) Jameson. Retired farm hand Erwin (Badger) Davis, although he kept his hand in now and again with farming, for beer money. Badger drank his beer in half pint glasses, the other card players always thought that was a bit odd. The youngster in the group was farmhand Garrett Devons. He would never change out of work clothes to go the pub. The others didn't take too kindly to Garrett's appearance at first, but they were used to it now. He smoked a lot, games were often disrupted while he went outside for a cigarette, much to the annoyance of Jules. The fourth card player was Norman (Norm) Prince who worked for the local undertaker. Norm's tipple was a glass of red wine.

'They buried poor old Bessie Armstrong today,' Norm reported. 'We had her wooden overcoat ready for several years, brave old gal.'

'That's sad to hear,' chipped in Badger who turned toward the bar and called to Annie, 'Hey Annie why have you fenced off the corner of the car park? Won't you need the space when the tourists start arriving?'

The blood seemed to drain out of Annie's face from that question, she went very pale and looked aghast.

'The ground in that corner of the car park has been getting very wet recently, like a marsh at times, I can't afford any tourists' cars to get stuck,' exclaimed Annie.

The four men stopped their card game and looked at Annie with inquisitive expressions. Then Annie blurted,

'You have no idea how much grief that could cause.'

At that point Badger's half full, half pint of beer, slid slowly off the table and fell to the floor and smashed.

'I didn't touch it,' cried Badger.

Two of the men got up from the table to help clear the mess when Norm's red wine flew off the table and smashed into the fireplace.

Jules bellowed, 'What the hell!' and started to move away from the table.

Suddenly all the lights went out in the pub. Monica let out a scream. Everyone stood still and motionless as the only light was the flicker of the fire.

CHAPTER 3 – THE CELLAR

Albert Baines was born to a Gentleman's Gentleman and a Pont. His father Wilber Baines was of the title Gentleman's Gentleman, he would groom the Lord of the Manor's horse and accompany him on his rides across the local countryside. When the Lord wasn't at home Wilber would be head stable boy. Wilber and his wife Agnes lived in a rented cottage on the estate. Agnes title was a Pont. She worked on the nearby flat-bottomed ferry roping visitors to and from the Estate's Country Park. She was paid a pittance, but it was an easy life. She would set up a tent on the riverbank and her children would set up camp there, but most of the time she had nothing to do but entertain her children.

Bert was one of four children. Edgar, his eldest brother, emigrated to New Zealand although he did return home for Bert's funeral. His other brother Arthur was acclaimed to be the clever child in the family. He won a scholarship at a London University and never returned to the Lake District. Bert lost touch with Arthur, who unfortunately never attended Bert's funeral.

His younger sister Gladys was always close to Bert, and often stayed at Ye Olde Elm Tree with Bert and Annie. She would take with her, the love of her life, her dog, Butch. Sadly, Gladys never made it to Bert's funeral either. She had been killed in a road accident. It happened at Ye Olde Elm Tree. Bert and Annie had been living at the pub for not quite a year; when her dog Butch ran across the road, having seen a shadow of a small boy. Gladys ran out into the road after

Butch and was hit by Farmer Forde's truck. His front and back wheels ran over poor Gladys, she stood no chance of surviving. Farmer Forde became a regular to the pub thereon, it was if he wanted to make amends in some way to Bert.

Bert met Annie at a local dance. Too shy to ask her out at first, it took three meetings before Bert would pluck up the courage to ask her to dance. They were married in 1946. Post war times meant rationing was still in existence, so despite a church wedding, their reception afterwards was quite a modest affair. It was at Annie's parent's house, tea and ginger cake.

Their honeymoon that followed, was all of three nights. They stayed in an old coaching inn called The Bull. They had a bedroom with a four-poster bed. Bert in later life would boast to some of his locals how he would chase Annie around that four-poster bed, but that was another story.

It was at The Bull that Bert got the taste for running a public house. In just three days he asked an endless number of questions to the bar staff and management. Bert even talked his way into the pub cellar to see for himself how the coordination of the beers and sundries came together. When Bert and Annie were first married, they lived with Annie's parents. Bert found himself work as a barman in a busy town pub. Annie hated the hours, Bert wouldn't get home until the early hours of the morning most nights, but he loved it, he was a natural publican.

At Ye Olde Elm Tree, in winter months, Bert had just two cask ales on the bar. He would double that once the tourist season started. During peak season five ales, sometimes even six. Ye Olde Elm Tree was classified a wet sales business. They never bothered much with food, despite growing a lot of their own vegetables in the pub garden. Sandwiches, pork pies, pasties, crisps or nuts, take it or leave it attitude. It stayed that way after Bert died. Annie stayed at the pub, she was distraught at first, poor Bert's death was so tragic, but she had grown into pub life.

It was a Monday morning, Bert had a routine, it was pipe cleaning in the cellar after a busy weekend. The day started with a cup of coffee and then a walk around their garden with Chester their Cavalier King Charles Spaniel. They would inspect the fishpond, most of the fish were up on the top looking for oxygen and food.

'The fish are looking good this morning Chester,' said Bert. Chester would wag his tail, maybe he did understand what Bert was saying.

The weather forecast was quite hot that day, but that was not gratifying for Bert as he would have his work cut out in the cellar. Five cask ales, two lager lines and two cider lines to flush and clean. Annie cooked him a Monday morning breakfast, all part of the routine, three rashers of bacon, three sausages, two fried eggs and grits. Bert learned to like grits following a short holiday in New Orleans. Annie wasn't keen. Crushed, ground corn, grits are awfully bland thought Annie. She enjoyed setting Bert up for the day on a Monday, with a hearty breakfast, then she would revert to tomatoes on toast for herself.

The cellar was through a trap door behind the bar and down a series of steps. Many locals thought it to be quite dangerous when a barrel needed changing during opening hours. Bert and Annie were used to it, leaving the trap door open whilst still serving. They had a young barmaid called Mollie who filled in from time to time. Mollie fell-down it once and ended up on her backside in the cellar below. She was shaken but okay, she did hurt her coccyx in the fall though.

On this Monday morning Bert was ready for the task in hand. Connecting a barrel at a time to water to flush the line clean. Flush with line cleaner, then flush water through once more to clean out the concentrated cleaner from the lines. Bert would be left with several buckets of pristine ale, flushed from the lines, much of which ended up down the drain. Bert always resented this and would pour off a few halves for himself. On this specific Monday morning, Bert had indulged in seven halves. He has nearly finished his chores. Chester would sit and watch Bert on a Monday morning, he would lay on a piece of old matting, that was his bed for the morning. Bert never knew what caused this to happen, but Chester let out a loud whimper and ran up the cellar steps, jumped onto the bar's wooden floor and ran off somewhere, still whimpering. The trap door slammed shut behind him. Stupid dog thought Bert. When the trap door was closed the cellar went quite dark despite there being an electric light in the cellar. Bert climbed up the steps to push the trap door open. He couldn't shift it, it seemed to be jammed shut. He called out several times,

'Annie, Annie. Can you hear me Annie?' No response.

I'll try later, thought Bert, I'll just clear up the cellar a little. Ah, I could try the cellar hatch to the car park, sometimes I forget to latch it from the outside, thought Bert. As Bert turned toward the bottom of the concrete steps, he seemed to slip on a grease gun he had used that morning. He fell very heavily and hit his head on a concrete plinth where the barrels were kept. Bert lay unconscious. It was then that the strangest thing happened; one by one, the beer barrel attachments slowly became detached. Barrel after barrel stated to pour on the cellar floor. There was a fresh water tap in the cellar, slowly that started to turn, cold water started to flow and then pour from the tap. The cellar started to flood quite quickly. For some strange reason, the single drain in the cellar floor was blocked. Bert laid unconscious head down on the cellar floor. The mixture of beer and water started to cover Bert. Bert let out a desperate gasp for air, but it was too late. Bert had drowned.

Later that morning Annie came to look for Bert. At first, she couldn't get the trap door open to the cellar, Chester watched her with a frown. One final tug before she would have to go and ask for help, when the door flew open. Annie ran down the concrete steps to see Bert submerged in dirty looking water. As she yanked him out, she could smell beer in the water. She pulled Bert up onto the steps, and soon realised he had taken his last breath. Chester watched from the top of the steps. How could this have possibly happened she asked herself?

Bert's tragic death silenced the pub for many weeks, months after. It took time for Annie and the locals to comprehend what had happened and how it had happened to poor Bert. It was Norm from the undertakers that broke the ice one night

'Well at least Bert drowned in his favourite beer,' he proclaimed.

CHAPTER 4 – THE VISIT

Annie telephoned her sister Nancy who lived near the coast, in Dorset. Nancy lived on her own in a two-bedroom apartment with a partial sea view, through a gap between two houses. She had separated from her husband Henry after their only son had left home and created his own independence. Nancy and Henry sold up their four-bedroom village property and each bought retirement apartments. Nancy had very little contact with her ex-husband and son afterwards; even the Christmas cards from them both, had come to an end.

'Hello,' answered Nancy.

'Hello Nancy, it's Annie, how are you?'

'Fine thanks Annie, how are you and how is that old haunted pub of yours?' Annie went silent. 'Hello, Annie, are you still there?' enquired Nancy.

Annie had no family now that Bert had died. The word haunted also grated on Annie.

'Do you fancy coming to stop for a few days before the tourist season starts?' asked Annie.

'Yes, that would be lovely,' replied Nancy, 'I tend to keep weekends free for WI work, as you know, but I could travel up on a Monday by train and travel back on the Friday.'

'Perfect,' said Annie and the two sisters agreed on a date. A late Monday arrival would provide Annie with the chance to do her cellar work. She loathed cellar work at first after Bert had mysteriously died. But over the two years that had passed, she was more hardened to it.

Nightmares at Ye Olde Elm Tree

Mary Ashcroft arrived at Ye Olde Elm Tree at 8.30 am. Mary was always punctual, never late for work. Mary was Annie's cleaner. She had cleaned at the pub, even before Bert and Annie took it on. She was a loyal employee to Annie and over the years had become her friend. Mary lived in a farm cottage on the Llewellyn Country Estate, at a peppercorn rent, thanks to the service her ex-husband gave to the estate. Mary's husband Royston walked out on her near on twenty years ago, they had no family. To this day she does not know where he is, or even if he is still alive. Annie liked Mary as she was old school. She would take on tasks such as cleaning out the Inglenook fireplace or polishing the pub's brass of her own accord. Mary would work mornings at Ye Olde Elm Tree, extra hours with the bedrooms during the tourist season. Afternoons she would allocate her time to just one room per day at the Llewellyn manor house. Annie was quite thrilled about her sister coming to stay; she asked Mary to prepare a bedroom for Nancy. Mary thought, Annie was quite excited that day, with her sister about to visit.

Nancy's journey up from Dorset was a long one, only one change though at Birmingham New Street station. Annie met Nancy at the local station in her Morris Minor. That night would be a quiet, planned chill at the bar, in Ye Olde Elm Tree. Monica was planning to join them. Monica loved it when Nancy visited. Time for some old-fashioned chitchat. In the bar that night Farmer Forde, reading his newspaper. In the snug, once called the smokers lounge, Eddie and Barbara. A middle-aged couple, who liked to canoodle in the peace and quiet away from the main bar. Annie would like to eavesdrop on them from time to time. A quiet Monday night all in all, three young village lads came in later in the evening, content to have a drink and play darts. Annie didn't know them very well, but she thought they were nice lads.

Tuesday morning Annie cooked eggs for herself and Nancy. Annie kept fourteen chickens at the bottom of the garden, so she was never short of eggs. Over breakfast Annie had blurt out to Nancy what had happened in the car park the other day.

'That's insane Annie,' said Nancy, 'have you not reported it to the authorities?'

'No Nancy,' Annie replied, 'I was too scared, terrified in fact. What if the police closed my pub down? What would I live on?'

'Yes, but Annie three men have been killed,' Nancy declared. 'In the most, insane circumstances. The whole affair sends shivers down my spine,' mumbled Nancy.

Annie stopped to gather her thoughts.

'There are still occasions when I think how the hell did it happen, or why did it happen, or did it happen at all?' Annie responded. 'If I report it to the police, it will soon be gossip, all around the county, country in fact, people will think I'm crazy!'

Nancy didn't know what else to say. Annie changed the subject,

'It's raining outside, how about some retail therapy in the local town?' she suggested. Nancy nodded with her approval.

Annie had asked her barmaid Mollie to cover for the week that Nancy was visiting. Mollie was able to work it around her other occupation of dog walking quite easily. The two ladies got ready then sped off to town in Annie's Morris Minor.

Tuesday evening was a normal evening at Ye Olde Elm Tree. Farmer Forde was in. The card school were in, creating as much noise as ever. Monica had turned up for another chitchat. A group of bikers dropped in for a couple of drinks. Desmond People and his lady friend Alice came in, both were estate agents. Annie did not care a great deal for Desmond, pompous, arrogant man, but a customer all the same. To make matters worse he insisted on joining in the conversation with Nancy and Monica.

Wednesday morning Annie pulled back the curtains to see a beautiful sunny day ahead of them. That's more like it she thought, the weather has been awful just of late. She walked around her grounds with Chester, she spoke to Chester the whole time, he was a real companion to Annie.

'The fish are looking good this morning Chester,' said Annie. If only dogs could talk? He might say where he had heard that before!

Annie stopped to look at an old lean-to on the back of the pub. Bert built it when they first arrived at the pub as cover for his motor bike. It was of a two upright beam construction with a galvanised steel roof, all fixed to the back wall of the pub. Annie never liked it. When it rained hard it would rattle down on that old tin roof, as she used to call it.

'I must get that old lean-to taken down Chester,' Annie said to her best companion. 'We should take it down before it falls down.'

Thanks to the nice weather, Annie & Nancy drove to a local lake.

'Let's take a boat trip to the other side of the lake,' Annie suggested.

'Ok but can I pay for it?' replied Nancy.

They really enjoyed the trip; spring was in the air. When they reached the other side, they decided to visit the nearby tea rooms. Both had a pot of tea, Annie had her favourite Eccles cake, Nancy had a big slice of the strawberry gateau. Conversation flowed freely, until Nancy approached the subject of the car park catastrophe.

'Have you thought any more Annie of going to the authorities about that car?' Nancy asked.

Annie looked daggers at Nancy for a moment then she replied,

'I don't know what to do. I do not think I can handle the press swarming all over the place, onlookers too, then what the hell would follow afterwards?' she asked. 'Would the pub get a bad reputation? Would I have any customers left?' Her voice started to go hoarse. 'Come on Nancy, drink up your tea, let's get heading back,' Annie said with a sense of purpose.

Wednesday evening was a busy one at the pub. Farmer Forde was in, no Monica that evening but it was darts night. Ye Olde Elm Tree were home to the Newcombe Arms. The district darts league requires a minimum of four and a maximum of ten per team. On this night there were seven per team, plus partners and friends, it was busy and loud.

Thursday was overcast. Annie took Nancy on a river walk then stopped off at a Petting Farm. It was lambing season. The highlight for Nancy was helping to bottle feed two baby lambs, one with colostrum and the other slightly older lamb, with milk.

Thursday evening was quiz night at Ye Olde Elm Tree. Alfie Richardson was a retired postmaster, he always organised the quiz for Annie, he loved it. He brought along his PA all very professional. Farmer Forde was in. So was his neighbouring farmer Granville. Monica was back, as it was to be Nancy's last night at the pub. Desmond People turned up again, without Alice that night. He seemed entranced by Nancy! There were five quiz teams, all in all a good night. Annie went to bed that night, she could not sleep and had to get up early next morning to take Nancy to the station. She kept going over in her mind that disastrous event with the car, but what made it worst Nancy had gone all day and all night without mentioning it. Annie really needed to talk about it to someone other than Nancy.

Friday morning, the ladies were up early to catch Nancy's train. Annie had made her some breakfast wraps to take with her. They hugged each other on the station platform.

'I am seriously thinking of going to the police Nancy,' Annie said.

'I wish you would,' replied Nancy as she boarded her train.

The weekend came and went, still no word from Annie on the car park disaster. It was a Tuesday, card school night at the pub. No farmer Forde, he had apologised to Annie as he was away for a few days buying stock. No Monica either. Eddie and Barbara were in the snug. Other than that, there was the card school and a couple passing by who had stopped off for a drink.

Halfway through the evening young Garrett had gone outside for his one of many, cigarettes. He had wandered up the side of the pub and was admiring the back garden, studying what a big garden they had. There was a sudden creak, then another creak, Garrett turned round to see what it was. Then there was almighty crash. The lean-to had come away from the building. A cross-member beam had swung round and hit Garrett full on in the face. He laid unconscious.

It was Jules who came to look for Garrett, cussing him for timewasting. Jules suddenly noticed Garrett laid on his back, there was a lot of blood coming from his head wound.

'He must have been hit by that falling timber,' screamed Jules. He rushed back into the pub, 'Call an ambulance,' cried Jules. 'That old lean-to at the back of the pub has collapsed on top of Garrett. There's blood everywhere,' said Jules slightly exaggerating. Annie's face was filled with horror and shock.

An ambulance took Garrett away to the nearby hospital. His prognosis was Traumatic Brain Injury (TBI). Garrett was proclaimed dead at 6.05 am the following morning.

CHAPTER 5 – CONFESSION

Annie heard banging on the front door of the pub. It was just after 11 am the morning after. She had just come up from the cellar behind the bar so she couldn't see who it was. They banged again.

'Who can that be at this hour?' questioned Annie. They banged again. They are persistent, thought Annie but as she approached the front door, she could see it was the police.

As Annie opened the door the Police Officer asked, 'Annie Baines?'

'Yes,' replied Annie.

'I am Detective Inspector Rita Judd. This is Detective Sergeant Malcolm Roach,' announced the Officer. 'May we come in and ask you a few questions? It's regarding the accident here yesterday with Garrett Devons.'

Annie welcomed them both into the pub. Ironically, they all sat at the table where the card school normally sit. The officers politely turned down Annie's offer of refreshment.

'If it's ok with you Mrs Baines,' said DI Judd.

Annie interrupted, 'Please call me Annie.'

'Thank you, Annie,' acknowledged the Inspector. 'If it's alright with you we would like to see where Mr Devons' accident took place, once we have had a little chat.'

'No problem,' said Annie.

'What is your recollection of what happened yesterday evening?' asked DI Judd.

'Garrett was playing cards,' said Annie calm and collectively. 'They have a card school every Tuesday,' Annie continued,

'Garrett tends to smoke a lot, he went out for a cigarette, next thing I knew Julian went to look for him and came running back into the pub with the news there had been an accident.'

'Julian being Mr Jameson?' confirmed DI Judd.

'Yes Julian Jameson,' replied Annie. Whilst the conversations were ongoing DS Roach was taking notes.

'We will be sending a small team of forensic officers to inspect the murder weapon used a little later today.' stated DI Judd.

'Murder weapon!' shrieked Annie. 'Is he dead? Weapon! A lean-to joist!'

'Sorry,' said the Inspector. 'I use the term weapon, far too often in my profession. Let me re-phrase that, the object that injured Mr Devons, and yes he died at 6.05 am this morning.'

Annie's face turned a ghostly white.

'Mr Jameson told us that the lean-to was unsafe and should have been knocked down a long time ago,' claimed DI Judd.

'You've spoken to Julian and he said that?' exclaimed Annie.

'Yes, we met with Mr Jameson before we came here, he was at the hospital,' said the Inspector. 'Can we have a look at the lean-to now Annie?'

The three of them walked around the back of the pub to see the remains of the lean-to, twisted galvanised steel roof laying on the floor. Annie stared at the timber with the blood-stained marks on it. Annie didn't know but Chester had followed them out of the front door. He instinctively went straight to inspect that timber. Annie shouted,

'Chester, leave it alone,' grabbed his collar and dragged him back into the pub. DI Judd and DS Roach were whispering to each other when Annie returned. She tried to eavesdrop but couldn't hear what they were saying.

'Can you let us have a list of your regular patrons that were in Ye Olde Elm Tree yesterday evening Annie?' asked DI Judd. 'We are on our way to see the other card players now, a Mr Davis and Mr Prince. Mr Jameson kindly let us have their details.'

Annie just couldn't believe what was going on, she felt drained.

'The forensic team shouldn't be too long,' said the Inspector, as the pair started to walk back to their police car. 'We'll be in touch, thank you Annie,'' called DI Judd.

Annie watched the two officers open the car doors and suddenly shouted,

'Wait a moment! I have something else I need to tell you,' said Annie nervously. 'Would you like to come back inside the pub?'

The two officers followed her back inside Ye Olde Elm Tree, thinking it was related to Garrett Devons' accident. This time they accepted Annie's offer of refreshment. Annie told the officers how she had three visitors booked in to stay and provided the date. She explained how she was on her way up to the two bedrooms in the roof, with fresh towels, when she heard a vehicle pull into the car park. She could see them from the apex window. When she returned to the window, she was horrified, half the car had sunk into the ground. There was yelling, screaming. There was a sound of smashed glass, the driver had broken his car window, but the car was still sinking! The driver climbed out of his window, but he seemed to be sinking into the mud. The far corner of the car park had turned into, what looked like, a swirling bog. She carried on to explain,

'The driver was just swallowed up by the ground. Then the car sunk into the ground as well. They must have all died; buried alive!' Annie sobbed.

DI Judd and DS Roach could hardly believe what they had just heard. They both looked astonished and dumbstruck.

'Why haven't you reported this before?' asked the Inspector.

'I was terrified,' answered Annie. 'I was scared, of what might develop, scared of what would follow with the press, police, the media, nosy onlookers, my customers, would my pub have to close? How would I survive? What would happen to my business afterwards?' Annie then passed the two officers a national newspaper cutting of the three men, missing! Their names corresponded with the booking in the pub diary. The Inspector and the Sergeant were now convinced, this was real.

'Do you mind Annie, if Sergeant Roach and I have a separate discussion for a moment?' asked the Inspector. Following a quick conversation with DS Roach, she declared, 'We should like to take a look at that area of the car park, please Annie.'

Annie then blurted out, 'You must be extremely careful, that's why I have cordoned off the far corner of the car park. So that no one goes there.'

The two officers took a walk down to the sectioned off area of the car park. They both stared at the ground in amazement.

'In all my years of police work, I have never heard of anything so horrendous,' said DI Judd.

'Gov,' barked the Sergeant, 'In the station stores we have a new metal detector, top of the range Gear Tech MD-4030, deep sensitive, they claim.' The Inspector looked enquiringly at her colleague. 'If there is a car under the ground, we should be able to trace it with the metal detector,' suggested DS Roach.

DI Judd thought for a moment and then announced, 'Call it in Malcolm, let's get it down here.'

Once the metal detector had arrived, DS Roach took charge of it. He went alone walking over the area very slowly, carefully, very cautiously. Annie watched from the top window. She was frightful of what might happen next. The Sergeant went backwards and forwards across the area several times. There was nothing. Not a sound from the metal detector.

'That's strange, don't you think Guv?' DS Roach looked puzzled. He tested it in different spots of the gravel car park. Then he continued to dig up a fifty pence piece and a short rusty iron bar. 'So that's proof the metal detector is working okay Gov,' exclaimed the DS.

At that point Annie announced she had made them both another cup of tea. Sergeant Roach laid the metal detector against the wall, and they re-entered the pub. DI Judd had more questions for Annie.

'How often did you say the ground in the corner becomes wet and boggy?'

Annie looked pensively at the detective, 'It doesn't normally,' replied Annie.

During the tea break the ground where the metal detector stood became wet and slimy. The ground started to bubble and swirl around. A hand slowly appeared. On the hand you could see both bones and rotting flesh. It grabbed the metal detector and dragged it slowly into the ground, until it had disappeared altogether.

DI Judd leaned over to DS Roach and said,

'We best go back to the station and think about what we should do next. We'd better have a report on the Superintendent's desk before we go home tonight.' They both bid Annie farewell and returned to the police car.

'Wait a minute,' interrupted the Sergeant. 'I best grab the metal detector.' He ran over to spot where he left it. That's crazy he thought, it's disappeared; has it been stolen?

CHAPTER 6 – THE EXCAVATION

Early next morning Annie had a telephone call from Detective Inspector Judd. 'Good morning Annie, we have decided to excavate that new section of car park. There will be a contractor due to arrive at Ye Olde Elm Tree later this morning.'

'Will my customers still be able to use the car park?' Annie asked.

'Yes Annie, we will make provision for that,' replied the Inspector. 'Detective Sergeant Roach will be joining them to oversee the work.' DI Judd put the phone down.

She turned to her Sergeant and said, 'Make sure you phone me as soon as you find anything.'

DI Judd and Detective Chief Superintendent Raj Thackeray had decided that this was to be more of an excavation than a dig. After talking to the police contractors, she authorised the use of a Mini Digger, selecting the Micro 1-ton JCB8008. The digger turned up just after 10.30 am. DS Roach was already there waiting for it to arrive. Driver George Pullman unloaded the digger and set out a plan with the Sergeant on where and how best to dig. George was rather excited about the task in hand, he had never had a chance to dig up a buried car before with dead bodies inside! DS Roach had coned off an area of the car park for customers to park, which was filling fast, the nice weather had started to invite tourists to the local area. The reduced car park was soon quite full, the Sergeant was waving vehicles on, much to Annie's disgust.

2 pm, and the Sergeant's phone rang, it was DI Judd

'Anything yet Sergeant?'

'No Guv,' answered DS Roach, 'The dig has been somewhat slow as we have been careful, not knowing what the next dig will find. We are about three feet down and nothing yet.'

DI Judd decided that she should join them. Lunch time trade had finished and she had managed to park her police car next to Annie's Morris Minor.

'We've dug down as far as this mini digger can go,' said the Sergeant. DI Judd pondered for a moment.

'The Landlady claimed that the ground was like a swamp,' said the Inspector, 'What if the car had moved to another section of the car park? Let us dig over there,' pointing to an adjacent section. The dig continued to a similar depth, nothing. 'We best bring in larger plant tomorrow to carry on the work,' said the Inspector, in frustration.

Garrett Devons' brother Gresham was extremely angry at his brother's death. He blamed publican Annie for poor maintenance at the pub. He had read in the local press how the lean-to was considered unsafe. In fact, he was more than angry, he was eating up inside with rage. It was early in the morning, roughly 1 am, recalls Annie, when Gresham's vehicle, a very old Ford Escort drove up outside the pub. It was pitch black, just a dimly lit night light in the pub, Annie was in bed asleep. Gresham kept his side lights on so he could see what he was doing. He opened his boot, inside were four rocks. He threw each one at the downstairs pub windows; he smashed three of the windows, the other rock hit the woodwork with minimal damage. Gresham jumped back into his car and raced away into the night.

8 am next morning, Annie was on the phone to DI Judd explaining what had happened that night. Later that morning a forensic officer arrived and took the rocks away for finger-print testing and photographed a fresh tyre print outside the pub. Annie phoned Bob Truman, her local DIY man, she had another job for him to repair the windows.

The next morning, was turning out to be a busy one, the contractor turned up with a JCB 5CX Eco Backhoe Loader,

'This beast will find any cars down there,' claimed George. They dug all day, they even dug in more sections of car park, nothing, not a sign of any car or bodies. At the end of the afternoon DI Judd and her Superintendent were reaching the same conclusion. Had Annie concocted the entire story? Perhaps she had read the newspaper article about the missing men, put the entry in the pub diary and imagined the whole thing?

'What a waste of police time and money,' said DCS Thackeray in a disgruntled manner.

Gordon McLarty was a freelance photographer, for several local newspapers. Gordon moved down from Glasgow after his marriage had split three years previously. Gordon had been reading some of the articles on Ye Olde Elm Tree. He seemed quite interested. Accidental death of Garrett Devons, the police digging up half the pub car park. What was that all about, he thought? Then he found an article regarding the mysterious death of the landlord Albert

Baines. I might look for myself he thought, see if there is anything worth photographing.

That night seemed like a busy but normal night in the pub thought Annie. A Mr & Mrs Baldwin had booked a long weekend four-night stay in Ye Olde Elm Tree. Annie had taken two more bookings for rooms that day, so she was quite pleased. She did hope that this awful experience with the car park and the police wouldn't put people off staying at the inn. Mr & Mrs Baldwin checked in around 6 pm, fortunately the car park had been put back to some normality. They unpacked, went downstairs for a drink and left to find somewhere local to eat. The Baldwins were in a bedroom on the first floor, the same floor that Annie slept. Mollie was also staying in a bedroom on the first floor, she was helping with the bar that night. It was a darts league match against the Anchor. Always a busy night, great rivalry.

Mr & Mrs Baldwin had an early night, they were both exhausted from their lengthy journey from Leicestershire. It was gone midnight when Mrs Baldwin nudged her husband and tried to wake him.

'Ugh, what is it?' said Mr Baldwin with his eyes still closed.

Mrs Baldwin whispered, 'I can hear footsteps outside our bedroom door.' They lay still and listened. 'Here they are again,' breathed Mrs Baldwin.

The old inn was three hundred years old and most of the floorboards creaked. The footsteps seemed to travel from left to right, stop, then return right to left, right outside their bedroom door. What followed was silence. Then the footsteps could be heard again, same routine. Mr Baldwin thought he had better investigate. He very quietly unlatched the bedroom door, quietly turned the handle and opened the door. He looked onto the landing and called out 'Is there anybody there?'

Annie heard this and appeared out of her bedroom. 'Everything okay Mr Baldwin?' asked Annie.

'I thought I heard footsteps,' replied Mr Baldwin.

'Probably the wind,' said Annie, 'This old building does creak at times.'

Mr Baldwin smiled at Annie, said good night, and went back into his bedroom. The couple could hear voices for a while, they thought it sounded like Mollie and Annie discussing something. They couldn't hear the conversation, they noticed their voices became raised at one stage, almost arguing. A good hour had passed and the Baldwins had started to both doze off, when the footsteps started again. Mr Baldwin decided not to investigate this time. They both laid motionless, listening, Mrs Baldwin squeezed her husband's hand. Her heart was racing, her mouth was dry, she was frightened.

CHAPTER 7 – REVENGE

Early next morning, Bob Truman arrived at Ye Olde Elm Tree to measure the pub windows, to replace the broken glass. Annie heard Bob arrive, she opened the bedroom window, she was still in her dressing gown.

'Morning Bob,' called Annie.

'Ah, morning Annie, who the hell would break your windows?' he asked, 'Have you got yourself an enemy?'

'No idea,' replied Annie. 'There's been a lot of strange things happening around here recently.'

Bob went off to buy the glass and promised to return tomorrow to repair the windows.

Mollie left soon afterwards. Annie apologised to Mollie for raising her voice last night. She knew Mollie was trustworthy and it was stupid to question her on money missing from the till earlier in the evening. Unexplained happenings were beginning to get on top of Annie.

It was then that Mr and Mrs Baldwin came downstairs with their overnight bag and small suitcase, they had decided to check out.

'But why?' asked Annie. 'You have only stayed for one night and you were booked in for four, altogether.'

Mr Baldwin sputtered a little but told Annie that they had decided to drive further north and visit some of the Scottish Lochs. He thanked her for a very pleasant stay. Annie tried offering them a refund for the three nights they wouldn't be staying, but they wouldn't accept it. How very strange, thought Annie.

Gresham Devons was visiting his elderly parents. The conversation was centred around his brother Garrett. His mother could not stop sobbing, grieving for the loss of one of her two sons. Gresham was full of anger.

'I blame that old witch at the pub, the landlady Annie,' barked Gresham. 'That lean-to wasn't safe, it's all her fault.'

His father replied in a softly spoken tone,

'But Gresham, the police are not going to press charges, they considered it to be an accident. There will be a coroner's report of course but they may conclude accidental death.' His father shook his head in disbelief, 'Poor Garrett, so young,' he whispered.

'Well I'm not satisfied with accidental death,' cried Gresham. 'I'll take the law into my own hands if I have to.' He decided it was time to say goodbye to his parents; his father begged him not to do anything stupid.

Photographer Gordon McLarty was at his home office. He had discovered a few much older articles on Ye Olde Elm Tree. He had spent several hours looking through newspaper archives, one newspaper even let him look through some old microfiche films. He discovered that Albert Baines' sister Gladys was accidentally killed outside the pub, when she was hit by a farm truck. He learned of how landlord Albert Baines changed the pub name from the King's Arms. Then in researching the King's Arms he found an old article on John Covington, who had sunk into the ground, to waist height, then died of a heart attack.

Fascinating he thought. Gordon knew a young keen reporter called Nick Fitzsimons, who might be interested in cutting an article on the old pub, if only he could get some interesting photographs in the meantime.

DI Judd was office bound that morning. The Detective Chief Superintendent wanted to know the cost of the fiasco at Ye Olde Elm Tree, that is how he referred to it. DI Judd was checking contractor quotations and making telephone calls to gather cost information. She put a hand-written breakdown on the Superintendent's desk, as she did so she thought, he's not going to like this! She also had the task of updating ICMP, International Commission on Missing Persons, and the NCIC, National Crime Information Centre, with the negative result of the excavation at Ye Olde Elm Tree. Not a pleasant task, she thought.

A few days passed it was the funeral of Garrett Devons in his family's village church. Annie wasn't looking forward to it at all. Mollie offered to accompany Annie to the funeral. Both ladies draped entirely in black arrived at the church in Annie's Morris Minor. Gresham caught sight of them as they arrived, he was seething. Everyone was there; his family, the card school, naturally, many villagers and many locals from Ye Olde Elm Tree. Even DI Judd and DS Roach were there. A Christian service was held in the church followed by a burial in the church graveyard. Annie felt uncomfortable she felt a lot of eyes were peering at her. Her palms started sweating, her throat went dry. She tried not to look too many people in the eye, her eyes were fixed mostly on the ground. As they lowered the coffin, Annie looked up and it was as if everyone was looking at her and not the coffin. She felt as if she was about to faint, she was barely perceptible, she touched Mollie on the arm and started to move away from the gathering. Mollie followed her, a little bewildered. They walked back to Annie's car and drove off. The two police officers looked at each other scornfully. One person who did not take his eyes off the two ladies, was Gresham.

The wake for obvious reasons, did not take place at Ye Olde Elm Tree. They organised it at the Newcombe Arms in the High Street of the village where the Devons family lived. Annie's pub was empty that night. Just a few passers by early evening. With no customers to talk to, Annie called last orders, to herself, just after 10 pm. Turned off all the pub lights and went to bed.

Gresham Devons parked his Ford Escort fifty yards from Ye Olde Elm Tree in a small layby. He got out of his car and lit a cigarette. Smoking the cigarette his eyes were fixed permanently on the pub. He threw his stub to the ground and started walking toward the pub, it was 2 am in the morning. He slowly walked around the pub until he was stood in the very spot where his brother was killed. Bob Truman had tidied up the area for Annie however Gresham remembered exactly where the lean-to used to be. He thought to himself, what damage could he do to revenge the old bitch. He shone a torch across the garden, he'd forgotten what a large garden it was. He thought he saw something move, like a shadow of a person, like a silhouette. He flashed his torch at the spot but couldn't see anything. Then his eyes fixed on the garden shed. I bet that's where Annie keeps most of her gardening tools he thought, he could set fire to it! He quietly walked over to the shed. He was conscious that the pub kept a dog, who might hear him stalking.

To his surprise the shed door wasn't locked. He shone his torch inside; tools, paints, an old chair, fertilisers, lawn food, rags, petrol can, this lot would make a fine blaze Gresham thought to himself. He took his lighter out of his pocket, when he thought he heard a noise behind him. He turned, with his back to the shed and flashed his torch in the direction he thought the noise had come from. Nothing there, he told himself. His mind had started to play tricks on him. Suddenly Gresham fell to ground in excruciating pain, he had been stabbed in the back by a garden fork. One spike had impaled his neck, the other three spikes had impaled the centre of his back, one of those spikes had clearly punctured his lung. Gresham was gasping for breath. As he fell, he dropped his torch, it landed three feet away and shone in the direction of the shed. He tried to reach his torch, but he couldn't. He tried to turn his head toward the shed, but he couldn't. He could hear the dog barking from inside the pub. He seemed pinned to the ground, face down, as if some force, like a foot, was pushing down on the garden fork.

CHAPTER 8 – THE FINDING

Annie was woken by Chester's barking; she looked at the clock, it was 2.25 am. She ventured downstairs, searched the pub to see if she could see anything wrong.

'What's got into you Chester? Did you hear something?' asked Annie. She went to the back door and unlocked it. She peered out into the garden. The night was still, dark, it was overcast, heavy cloud. She shut the door, locked it, then decided to give Chester some of his favourite biscuits. Whatever it was that spooked Chester he forgot all about it and got tucked into his biscuits. Annie went back to bed.

Mary Ashcroft arrived at Ye Olde Elm Tree at 8.30 am as punctual as ever. When she arrived that morning, Chester was up and restless, almost irritated, agitated.

'What's up Chester?' Mary asked. Normally Mary would walk through the back door and Chester would raise his head in acknowledgement that the day was about to start and wag his tail. Not this morning. There was no sign of Annie yet, so Mary switched the kettle on and let Chester out into the garden to do his business. Chester ran straight over to the shed, where he started barking, he did not let up, he continued barking. Mary went to investigate what was wrong. She let out a scream. Annie arrived in her dressing gown having heard Mary's scream. They both stood over the dead body.

'What a horrible way to die,' bawled Mary. 'Do you know him?' she asked.

Annie took a big breath 'Yes I know him,' she replied. 'The lad that was killed by the lean-to recently,' there was a pause, 'It's his brother. Gresham Devons.' Tears started to roll down Annie's cheeks, she was distraught.

Detective Inspector Judd took a call from Annie informing her of their findings.

'Annie, don't touch anything,' instructed the Inspector. 'We'll be over straight away with a forensic team.' The Inspector knocked on the door to Detective Chief Superintendent Thackeray and detailed the conversation she had just had with Annie.

'Grab your hat Rita, let's get over there PDQ,' said the DCS.

Brigit arrived at Ye Olde Elm Tree shortly afterwards. Brigit was a larger than life character, with a wicked sense of humour. One to stand out in a crowd, with her black curly hair, orange make-up and often tight-fitting clothes. Brigit would collect the laundry after the weekend, she would always return it, ironed and in pristine condition. Annie and Mary both loved Brigit, she would often arrive with a joke or a wisecrack, looking for laughs. Not this morning; both Annie and Mary were too upset over the grotesque discovery of Gresham Devons' dead body.

Photographer Gordon McLarty telephoned his reporter friend Nick Fitzsimons.

'Hello, Nick Fitzsimons, can I help you?'

'Aye Nick, it's Gordon, I may have something interesting for you to research.'

Nick became intrigued. 'I hope it's not a foolish errand, like the last one,' replied Nick. He was referring to a sighting on the nearby hillside, that never materialised.

'No Nick,' answered Gordon. 'There is this pub called Ye Olde Elm Tree; there has been a lot of strange things going on there recently. There was an accidental death of a young farm hand, a lean-to fell on him. The police have been digging up half the car park, so say, they were looking for three missing men. If you go back in time, the landlord died mysteriously in his cellar, his sister killed by a truck outside the pub. All a bit weird if you ask me.' What Gordon did not know was what had happened to Gresham Devons in the early hours of the morning.

'Now you come to mention it, it does all sound like a potential story. I had heard about the accident and that ludicrous excavation of the pub's car park, what a waste of police time,' answered Nick.

'I am thinking of popping over there later, see if I can get a few good photos,' replied Gordon.

'Ok Gordon keep me posted,' said Nick.

'Aye I will,' said Gordon and put the receiver down.

Ye Olde Elm Tree car park looked like a battle scene. Blue lights flashing, police cars, ambulance, a forensic team on hand. Gresham Devons' body was very carefully moved onto a stretcher, then into the ambulance. His body was kept face down. DCS Thackeray insisted that the garden fork was to be removed in the forensic laboratory, which meant they could not use the standard body bag, quite unorthodox.

DCS Thackeray and DI Judd entered Ye Olde Elm Tree to ask Annie and her cleaner Mary a few questions. Brigit made herself scarce with the police presence there. Annie explained how she heard her dog Chester barking at 2.25 am, fed him and went back to bed. Then she explained how she heard Mary let out a scream from the garden next morning and rushed downstairs to investigate. Mary explained what time she had arrived at the pub and how the dog was restless, so she let him in the garden.

'It was the dog that found the body,' declared Mary.

'Annie,' questioned DI Judd, 'How well did you know Gresham Devons?'

'I have known him for years,' answered Annie. 'Not that well though, his local was the Newcombe Arms. His brother Garrett was more of a regular,' stated Annie.

'I saw Gresham staring at you Annie, at his brother's funeral,' DI Judd implied. 'Why was that, do you think?'

'I can only presume it was over his brother's accident,' said Annie. 'I loved that lad Garrett, like a son,' she replied.

'What do you think Gresham Devons was doing in your garden at 2.25 am in the morning?' asked the Inspector.

'I have no idea,' exclaimed Annie, 'but I wouldn't be surprised, if it were Gresham who broke my windows the night before!'

Bob Truman turned up with the glass to repair the windows. This is pandemonium he thought: blue lights, ambulance and police cars. He could not drive his truck into the car park. A constable approached him and asked him to move on.

'What's going on officer?' Bob asked.

'There has been an accident. Kindly move on sir,' the constable replied.

'But I've got glass on my truck to repair the broken pub windows,' claimed Bob.

The police officer checked Bob's truck, looked at the broken windows and said, 'Wait a minute please sir.'

The constable walked into the pub to consult with DI Judd. On his return the constable said,

'You can carry on repairing the windows. Can you park your truck over there?' He pointed to a place away from the busy car park.

'The accident,' Bob responded, "Is Annie the landlady okay?'

'The licensee is fine,' came the constable's reply.

Ernie who normally arrived at Ye Olde Elm Tree with a beer dray, arrived with a transit van during the frenzied scene in the car park, with two boxes of bottled beers. These were for an out-of-stock cask ale at the depot, much to Annie's annoyance. The constable took the boxes from Ernie and stacked them in the pub porch; he was keen to move Ernie on quickly. Ernie drove off thinking, what the hell has happened.

Gordon McLarty had written up his research on Ye Olde Elm Tree and the King's Arms and had emailed it to his reporter friend, Nick Fitzsimons. He then drove to Ye Olde Elm Tree. On arrival he could not believe his eyes. What he saw in front of him looked haphazard. The same constable asked Gordon to move along.

'What's happened?' asked Gordon

'There's been an accident sir, so kindly move along,' the constable replied.

'Who was in the accident?' enquired Gordon.

'We are unable to say sir,' replied the constable. 'Now, if you would kindly move on. Thank you.' The constable's voice sounded more forceful.

Gordon drove off and parked fifty yards down the road, slightly out of sight; he had parked in the same layby where Gresham had parked his car in the early hours of the morning. Gresham's car was still there.

Gordon sneaked back to the pub and took a few photographs of the chaotic scene in Ye Olde Elm Tree car park.

'Excuse me sir,' shouted the constable.

Gordon acknowledged the constable with a wave and swiftly walked back to his car. Gordon felt excited; he had an adrenaline rush. I wonder what has happened, he thought.

Back at the Forensic Lab, the only fingerprints and DNA on the garden fork, was that of the landlady Annie Baines.

'Let's pull her in Rita,' said the Detective Chief Superintendent. 'Let's try some interrogation and see if we can learn any more from her.'

'And the charge sir?' asked DI Judd.

'Murder,' said the DCS, nodding his head.

At 4.45 pm DI Judd's police car parked outside Ye Olde Elm Tree. Sergeant Roach and the Inspector banged on the pub's front door. Annie was not surprised that they had returned so soon; she answered the door. She noticed the Detective Sergeant was holding handcuffs.

'Annie Baines,' said DI Judd in an authoritative voice. 'You are under **arrest** on suspicion of the murder of Gresham Devons. You **do** not have to say anything, but it may harm your defence, if you **do** not mention when questioned, something which you later rely on **in** court. Anything you do say, may be given in evidence.'

CHAPTER 9 – UNDER ARREST

Annie made sure everything was switched off, except the fridges, freezer, and the ice machine. She bent down and kissed Chester on the head.

'Mummy won't be long, those silly policemen have it all wrong,' said Annie to her best friend, her pet dog. It was as if Chester understood Annie, he gave her a sorrowful expression.

She grabbed the pub diary, mobile phone and shoved them into her handbag, locked up the pub and entered the police car, where the two officers drove her to the local police station for questioning. Annie was allowed three phone calls, she asked for four, but was told she could only have three. The first call was to her sister Nancy. She explained what had happened to Gresham Devons and the fact that she had been arrested.

'That's absolutely nuts,' bawled Nancy, 'Be strong Annie, don't let them bully you,' were her parting words.

The second call was to Mary, her cleaner. Both ladies were tearful on the telephone when Annie told Mary that she had been arrested. Annie asked Mary to look after Chester and contact Bob Truman and Mollie to let them know what had happened.

The third call was to a solicitor. Reginald Spearing was once an old friend of her late husband Bert. Close to retirement, Reginald shared a small office in town with two other partners. Annie explained what had happened and that she had been arrested.

'That's preposterous,' bellowed Reginald. 'Which station are they holding you? I will come over as soon as I can. The police can only hold you for up to 24 hours Annie, after that they can apply for an extension, 36 or 96 hours, but they would have to charge you, and I don't consider that they have the necessary evidence. Be cautious on what you say to them Annie, until I get there.'

Annie took the opportunity to check her pub diary before the police would confiscate it. She had a family called Delany booked in for the weekend, a married couple and their two sons taking up two rooms. If Reginald Spearing is correct, Annie prayed she would be back in the pub for the weekend. The darts team were playing away from home this week; that's fortunate thought Annie.

Being a publican, Annie never got to see much television. She must have watched a few police documentaries and thrillers, now and again, as nearly every question Detective Inspector Judd and Detective Sergeant Roach asked Annie, her answer was, 'No comment.'

Reginald Spearing arrived at the station. The first thing he did was insist on a glass of water for him and his client. DS Roach reluctantly obliged. Annie was drilled on her relationship with Gresham Devons, his late brother Garrett, even his parents, who Annie never really knew. Questioned on how many times Gresham had visited Ye Olde Elm Tree, in what circumstances? Was there a grudge? Why did she think it was Gresham who had smashed her pub windows the night before? She was questioned on what really happened at 2.25 in the morning, questioned about the garden fork. The police even revisited her husband's accidental death, which was totally irrelevant to the line of questioning, Reginald Spearing reminded them. Even her mental health was questioned over the missing men incident. Reginald had not heard anything about the car park trauma.

'May I have a moment alone with my client?' asked Reginald.

The officers agreed and the interview was terminated. Annie and her solicitor were informed that interviewing would reconvene at 10 am the following day. That would mean Annie would spend the night in a cell; she shuddered at the thought.

There were a few visitors to Ye Olde Elm Tree that evening to find out it was closed. Farmer Forde and his neighbouring farmer Granville almost arrived together. They had a discussion outside the pub on why it might be closed. Farmer Forde was quite mystified; he believed his newspaper that Annie always ordered for him, might be inside the locked pub, on the bar.

Bert and Annie were lessees of Ye Olde Elm Tree, and since Bert's tragic death Annie was the sole licensee. The pub company that owned Ye Olde Elm Tree property, inherited it from a previous pub company, they since owned over two thousand, five hundred hotels and public houses with just under one hundred area managers to oversee the businesses. Annie's lease was a twenty-year lease, quite rare in modern days, as shorter tenancy contracts were favoured more.

Annie's area sales manager was Charles Braithwaite. Annie was not keen on him, but she tolerated him. An ex-policeman, six foot plus, distinguished, grey trained back hair, handlebar moustache, wore on many occasions a pin stripe suit, tie or cravat, top pocket handkerchief. Annie always chuckled at his appearance whenever he asked to inspect the cellar. Charles was in his office reviewing the area's sales figures. He came across Ye Olde Elm Tree, no beer order for that current week. Strange he thought, especially as it is the start of the tourist season. Perhaps Annie had forgot to place her order. Perhaps something is wrong. He felt it was time to visit Ye Olde Elm Tree to investigate.

Gordon McLarty's mobile phone rang, it was his reporter friend Nick Fitzsimons.

'Hi Gordon, it's Nick, have you heard the latest? There has been a murder at Ye Olde Elm Tree.'

Gordon puffed his cheeks out, 'No, I witnessed a chaotic car park with police cars, ambulance, took a few hasty photographs, what has happened?' asked Gordon.

'Well the lad that was killed by the lean-to, Garrett Devons, his brother Gresham Devons has been murdered in the garden of Ye Olde Elm Tree,' informed Nick.

'That's crazy! His brother!' exclaimed Gordon.

'Yes, the police have arrested a woman, but we are not sure who she is at this stage, the police haven't divulged her name,' Nick replied.

'Bloody hell,' hollered Gordon. 'His brother! A woman! Was he married or possibly a girlfriend, what a story!'

'We are not sure of the circumstances,' answered Nick. 'What we do know is, he was stabbed in the back with a garden fork.'

'A garden fork, bloody hell,' wailed Gordon.

'Are you still planning to go down there and take some photographs?' asked Nick.

'Aye mate, I'm on my way,' answered Gordon. 'I reckon I can get over there for around 2 pm. I might get the chance to ask the landlady a few questions,' Gordon said with a cheeky smile; he had no idea.

'Great keep me posted Gordon, I might try and get down there myself, a little later,' Nick hung up the phone, feeling quite excited.

Gordon had a 1960'S Art Deco sliding door cabinet. He slid a door back, inside was his camera collection. He pulled out his pride and joy. A Canon EOS 90D Digital SLR camera. 18-135m lens, 4 k Ultra HD, WIFI, Bluetooth, Optical viewfinder, 3" angle touch screen. Gordon caressed his camera as he took it out of the cabinet. He would never be allowed to own something so beautiful, if he were still living in Glasgow, still married. But now, as a single man.

Gordon drove impatiently to Ye Olde Elm Tree. He arrived just before 2 pm. He wanted to interview the landlady, but the pub was closed. That is strange he thought. He banged on the front door, no response. Gordon received a text just then, from Nick, apparently Gresham's car is still parked fifty yards up the road from Ye Olde Elm Tree. Gordon walked up the road and photographed Gresham's car. He walked back toward the pub's gravel car park. He had flashbacks of the last time he photographed the car park, ambulance, police cars, pandemonium. Now it was a silent empty car park, apart from an old Morris Minor. He took photographs of the car park. Gordon ventured around the side of the building. He photographed where the lean-to had once stood. He knocked on the backdoor. No answer.

What is going on, he thought, the pub should be open? He wandered into the garden, taking shots of the pub. Big garden, he thought, the pub should make more use of this much land. Gordon decided to go down to the bottom of the garden, to take a panoramic photograph. He wondered where Gresham had been killed. He looked around but there were no clues. He wandered down to the old elm tree at the bottom of the garden. He did not know of the significance of that old tree, how Bert named the pub after it, and that Bert used to often have his lunch underneath that tree, on a warm sunny day, sometimes hearing voices.

This is a great place to take a wide photograph of the garden, he thought. He took several photos. Gordon stood on the grass, but as he moved his foot, he noticed the grass had become very squelchy. He stepped aside to what he thought was a drier section. Gordon seemed to sink further as the ground was becoming saturated. He tried again to step aside. This is getting worse he thought. Water was covering his trainers. I need to find a dry piece of grass he thought. Suddenly an arm appeared and grabbed his left leg around his shin and calf. Gordon looked down at the hand, horrified, it was part bone, part flesh. Goodness knows why, he tried to photograph the hand. A yank on the other leg, may have prevented the perfect photograph. A second hand had grabbed his right leg. This hand was covered in green slime. The two hands started to pull Gordon into the ground.

'What the hell is happening,' he yelled. A third hand appeared and grabbed the back of Gordons jacket. He fell backwards. He dropped his camera.

'Help, help, help me,' he shouted. Gordon was slowly getting dragged into the ground. He screamed for someone to help him, but there was no one there to hear him. Gordon disappeared below the ground. Water swirled around, a few air bubbles appeared, then it went still and silent. Gordon's camera sat on the waterlogged grass.

CHAPTER 10 – THE CONSEQUENCE

Detective Chief Superintendent Thackeray and Detective Inspector Judd met to review Annie's arrest. The only evidence they had after the interrogation was Annie's fingerprints on the murder weapon. But it was Annie's garden fork, there were no other prints.

'It's not enough to hold her for any longer,' explained DI Judd 'We are going to have to let her go.'

The Superintendent agreed and nodded in favour of releasing her. 'We have not learnt anything from interrogating her, have we Rita?' asked the Superintendent.

'Sadly, no,' replied the Inspector. Annie Baines was released from custody at 2 pm. Her solicitor Reginald Spearing escorted Annie out of the police station and drove her back to Ye Olde Elm Tree.

'The press may bother you now Annie,' said Reginald. 'They are likely to offer you significant sums of money for your story. My advice, in situations like this, is to write down what you are comfortable to tell them. Then when they contact you, always try and speak to them by telephone, never in person. When they ask you questions, refer to your notes, or read from them if it's better to do that.' Annie thanked Reginald and gave him a big hug. She was home.

She rang Mary with the news. Mary thought that was fantastic news; she said she would bring Chester home in the morning. Another night away from Chester, that made Annie feel sad.

She rang her sister Nancy, 'Annie I'm happy to jump on the next train to come and stop with you if you need company,' said Nancy. Annie thanked her and promised to keep in touch.

'Oh hell,' uttered Annie, she had forgotten to place her beer order! She phoned the pub company straight way with an emergency order.

A car drew up outside. The driver leaned over to see if the pub was open. Looks closed he thought, and drove on.

Nick Fitzsimons arrived at Ye Olde Elm Tree. He knocked the front door, Annie answered.

'Good afternoon Mrs Baines,' Nick introduced himself, with his business card. Was this to be the first of the press to approach me? she thought. Nick was enquiring if Annie had seen his photographer friend Gordon McLarty and explained how he was planning to visit the pub to take photographs.

Annie answered, 'Sorry, I haven't seen him; I've been away.' Nick tried to press Annie on the Gresham Devons' murder. 'I'm afraid, the matter is in the hands of the police. I can't help you with your enquiries, I'm sorry.' said Annie. Nick looked dejected, downcast, he so wanted to present a story to his editor, regarding Ye Olde Elm Tree.

Charles Braithwaite was in his office and noticed that Annie's beer order had arrived. He was relieved, although, he should still pay her a visit he thought.

Nightmares at Ye Olde Elm Tree

Annie ventured into her garden. She stopped and stared at where the lean-to once stood and dropped her head, as if in prayer. Annie walked over to the shed. Her eyes fixed on the spot where they found Gresham; she shook her head in bemusement. Then out of the corner of her eye, she caught sight of a camera laying on the grass, near the old elm tree, at the bottom of the garden. She walked toward it and nearly picked it up when she stopped, and thought, fingerprints! It looked expensive, she thought, then the penny dropped, the reporter that called earlier was asking after a photographer, perhaps it belonged to him?

Annie telephoned DI Judd and explained how she had a visit from a reporter looking for a photographer, now she has just discovered an expensive camera in her back garden.

'Have you touched it?' asked the Inspector.

'Are you kidding?' retaliated Annie. 'Put my fingerprints on it, you must be joking.' DI Judd promised to send an officer round to pick it up. As she hung up the phone, the Inspector hoped they did not have another missing person at Ye Olde Elm Tree.

The Delany family arrived at Ye Olde Elm Tree just before 4 pm. On the booking, Mrs Delany asked if her teenage sons could have a separate room, far away from their parents. Strange request thought Annie at the time. She booked Mr & Mrs Delany on the first floor at the front of the pub, the boys a roof room in the loft overlooking the back garden.

Annie took a phone call from the editor of the Star News.

'Mrs Baines, my name is Colin Coombes, editor of the Star News.' The line went silent. Oh god, thought Annie, this may be the first of the invasive phone calls from the press.

'Hello Mr Coombes, how can I help you?' said Annie, calm and collected. Colin Coombes went on to tell Annie that his newspaper would offer five thousand pounds for her story regarding the death of the two Devons brothers. Annie thanked the editor and promised she would think about it and get back to him. He was frustrated by Annie's response and elected to call her back, first thing in the morning.

Annie took a second call. 'Hello, Ye Olde Elm Tree,' said Annie.

'Is that Mrs Baines the landlady?' asked the caller.

'Yes, this is Mrs Baines,' came the reply.

'Good afternoon Mrs Baines, my name is Grayson Attenborough, editor of the Rayleigh Daily Standard. Our newspaper would be interested in representing your story on what may have happened to Garrett and Gresham Devons at Ye Olde Elm Tree.' Annie listened to what the editor had to say, when she told him that she had already received an offer from another newspaper.

'How much did they offer you Mrs Baines? If you do not mind me asking?' came his response.

'Five thousand pounds,' said Annie, confidently.

'We will double it,' said Grayson Attenborough. Annie was flabbergasted. She told the editor she would like to sleep on it and thanked him very much for the telephone call.

Nightmares at Ye Olde Elm Tree

Annie telephoned Colin Coombes at the Star News. She explained how the Rayleigh Daily Standard had offered her double for her story, ten thousand pounds. The line went silent.

'We can double that Mrs Baines, twenty thousand pounds, but that will have to be our final offer.' Annie accepted the offer. She notified the Rayleigh Daily Standard of her decision.

Grayson Attenborough said when hearing the other offer,

'I'm afraid, our newspaper would not be able to match such a sum.' Annie had just one hour before she had to re-open the pub. She remembered the advice of Reginald Spearing and sat down in the pub office, upstairs. Annie should write down what she would be comfortable saying to the newspaper.

It was 6 pm, opening time, Annie was not looking forward to this. Farmer Forde was the first to arrive. He sat in his usual spot, but there was no newspaper to read! Annie sincerely apologised and then went to great lengths to explain her ordeal in the police station over the last two days. He was very understanding.

Estate agents Desmond People and his girlfriend Alice popped in for a drink to acquire the latest gossip. Annie explained the events in detail.

'Were you arrested?' asked Alice.

'No,' replied Annie. 'Just helping the police with their enquiries.' That was a little white lie, Annie thought.

Detective Sergeant Roach entered Ye Olde Elm Tree, just before 7 pm; he called in on his way home from the station.

The conversation stopped when he walked in the bar, in full uniform.

'Good evening,' said the Sergeant, 'I believe there is a camera to collect?'

'Ah yes,' said Annie, 'Follow me.' Annie led the Sergeant into the back garden. They walked down to the old elm tree, where Annie pointed out the camera. DS Roach fetched from his pocket a pair of disposable latex gloves, put them on, picked up the camera, bagged it for his forensic department and wished Annie a pleasant evening. When Annie returned to the bar, everyone wanted to know what that was all about.

'Just some newspaper photographer came snooping around earlier, taking photographs of the pub and garden and left his camera behind,' said Annie in a self-assured manner.

'A photographer! Left his camera behind!' exclaimed Desmond People. 'You just can't get the staff these days,' he said in a joking fashion.

Monica was next to arrive at Ye Olde Elm Tree. She was impassioned on hearing the gossip. Annie was happy to oblige and kept the story of just helping the police with their enquiries. By 9 pm Annie asked a busy bar if they could change the subject of conversation, she was feeling exhausted and nauseous.

The Delany boys, Luke, fifteen and Jack, thirteen had settled down for the night in the top bedroom. It was approximately 2 am when the youngest brother thought he could hear his name being called, from outside in the garden. I must be hearing things, he thought. The sound came again,

'Jack, Jack.' His eyes were wide open by now. Jack got out of bed and stared out into the garden. The moon was at a waning gibbous stage, in a cloudless sky, which lit up the garden. Jack's eyes widened. He thought he saw a man in the form of a shadow, silhouette, crouching, quite badly. The figure seemed to disappear behind the tree at the bottom of the garden. He stared for a while; must be seeing things now he thought.

Seconds later another shadow of a child, which also disappeared by the tree. He watched eyes glued, then before him, a third figure, shadow, another man, more upright than the first man. The figure walked toward the tree, stopped, and turned to face the back wall of the pub. It was then, Jack thought the figure was looking directly at him! Can he see me? Jack asked himself. He dropped down below the window, moved quickly away from the window, crawled along the floor, and jumped back into bed, pulling the bed covers over his head.

CHAPTER 11 – BREAKING NEWS

Annie was up early to cook the Delany family's breakfast. Three English breakfasts for Mr Delany and his two sons. Cereals and fruit for Mrs Delany. Mary arrived shortly afterwards with Chester who received the biggest hug from Annie. Young Jack had little appetite, he hardly touched his breakfast, which concerned his mother.

Charles Braithwaite cooked himself two boiled eggs and toast for breakfast. About to crack the first egg open, he read the morning paper headlines. 'BROTHERS KILLED AT YE OLDE ELM TREE'. Charles read the report with bated breath. He could hardly believe his eyes. He was due to make sales calls in a different direction to Ye Olde Elm Tree, he needed to re-direct his plans for the day.

It was just before 9 am Annie took a call from the newspaper, Star News.

'Hello, is that Mrs Annie Baines?' asked reporter Godfrey Wallace. Editor Colin Coombes had assigned Godfrey to interview Annie for her story; he was considered by the editor, a top-class reporter.

'Yes, this is Mrs Baines,' came the answer.

Godfrey asked if he could call in on her at Ye Olde Elm Tree, within the hour, for an interview.

'Sorry Mr Wallace,' said Annie 'I'll only carry out the interview over the telephone.' She remembered what Reginald Spearing had recommended.

That's quite an unorthodox request Mrs Baines,' replied the reporter. 'We always conduct our interviews face to face.'

Annie explained that her legal representation insists on conducting it that way.

'Can I call you back momentarily, I will need to clarify that with my editor,' asked Godfrey. Annie agreed, hoping that a telephone interview would not impact on her fee.

Bob Truman arrived at Ye Olde Elm Tree and parked his pick-up truck next to Annie's Morris Minor. Annie met him with a mug of tea.

'Morning Annie, ah that's very welcome, it's a bit nippy this morning,' said Bob rubbing his hands together. 'What a terrible ordeal for you Annie, two brothers killed here, in such a short space of time.'

Annie and Bob held a heartfelt discussion on the recent phenomenon at Ye Olde Elm Tree. Annie considered Bob a good friend, who was always at hand when needed. Annie asked Bob if he would erect a fence from the back wall of the pub, to the back wall of the car park. She wanted to close off any access to the pub's back garden. Bob measured up for the work.

Godfrey Wallace called Annie back. Annie brought up the subject of the fee. Godfrey asked her for her bank details so they could transfer the fee after the interview; that put Annie's mind at rest. The telephone interview lasted just over an hour. Godfrey asked a lot of really searching questions, Annie kept referring to her notes. After the interview Annie thought the reporter had not gained any more than the police did, although she did have three concerns. Godfrey questioned Annie intensely over the missing men, car tragedy. She felt he would build his story on that awful experience. She had agreed for a photographer from his newspaper to photograph the exact locations where Gresham had been murdered and Garrett had been accidentally killed. She regretted letting it slip, that the remains of the lean-to had been taken away because it was not safe. Annie slumped in a chair afterwards to reflect the protracted conversation, she hated reporters and their clever manipulative ways.

DI Judd took a call on her mobile phone. 'Hello Detective Inspector Judd,' asked the caller.

'Speaking,' replied the Inspector.

'It's Doctor Sylvia Huntley here from the forensic laboratory. We have the photographs from the Canon camera developed.'

'That's good,' replied DI Judd. 'Is there anything incriminating in the photographs?'

The Doctor paused to answer the question. 'Not really, although the final photograph taken is quite a mystery, it is probably best you come over to the lab and have a look for yourself,' answered Dr Huntley.

'I'll try and get to you, late afternoon,' suggested DI Judd.

'Fine, see you then,' confirmed the Doctor.

Charles Braithwaite arrived at Ye Olde Elm Tree approximately 1.30 pm; it was extremely busy, he found one of the few parking places in the car park. This is amazing he thought, he had never seen it so busy. Charles took out his briefcase, locked his car, straightened his top pocket handkerchief and walked into the pub through the front door. Annie had to ask Mollie to help-out on the bar as it was so busy. Charles edged past a few customers to get to the bar. He smiled at Annie.

'When is my emergency beer order going to arrive?' she asked him, rather abruptly. 'You can see how busy we are.'

'Tomorrow morning,' he replied. 'I was hoping to have a conversation with you about the deaths that have occurred here,' he said hastily.

'No chance Charles,' replied Annie. 'Why don't you phone me after 3 pm once I have got rid of all these noisy customers.' Charles agreed but he emphasised to Annie, that his directors would soon be looking for answers on what has been going on at Ye Olde Elm Tree. Charles negotiated his way through the crowded bar and left through the front door.

'Bloody landlords,' Annie muttered under her breath.

Charles returned to his car. There was a message on his answer phone. The pub company had called a directors meeting on Monday morning; Charles was asked to attend to update the board on the trading position of Ye Olde Elm Tree.

It was a Saturday morning in New Zealand. Bert's eldest brother Edgar Baines was reading a national paper. His eyes suddenly fixed on a report on the death of two brothers in a public house, North England, called Ye Olde Elm Tree. He read on; one brother had been murdered with a garden fork, the other died of head injuries from a fallen lean-to. Then to his astonishment, he read landlady Annie Baines had been arrested. Edgar could not believe Annie would have anything to do with a murder! He could not get the thought out of his head all day, that day. Maybe he should jump on the next aeroplane to the UK?

Charles Braithwaite telephoned Annie at 3.30 pm.

'Hello Annie, Charles here, how are you coping with everything that has happened? Have the police said why they arrested you?'

'Oh, hello Charles, my fingerprints were on the murder weapon,' she replied. 'Big deal, it's my bloody garden fork,' Annie said with a sense of irritability. 'How am I coping?' She thought carefully. 'Best I can Charles. I had to shut the pub for 24 hours, while I was arrested, but business has been booming since I re-opened. With the pub being in the news, so many visitors, or should I say bunch of snoops! You say I have an emergency beer delivery in the morning, well I might need another soon, if this keeps up.'

That was music to Charles' ears, sales on the increase.

'Annie, Monday morning I have to attend a board meeting to inform them on events at Ye Olde Elm Tree,' declared Charles. 'Should anything new materialise can you please let me know?'

Charles gave Annie his mobile telephone number. He has never done that before thought Annie. She agreed and hung up the phone. She contemplated for a few seconds, meddling, interfering pub company was her observation.

DI Judd entered the forensic department building, signed in on a register, and proceeded to walk toward the laboratory where Dr Sylvia Huntley worked.

'Good afternoon Inspector,' Dr Huntley greeted DI Judd. She took the Inspector over to her office. 'The photographs are all of Ye Olde Elm Tree, crowded car park, with an ambulance and police cars, an empty car park. Photographs of the pub from the front, the side and the back. Several photographs of the garden. I checked though he did not take a photograph of the spot where Gresham Devons died. Perhaps he never knew where that was,' reported Dr Huntley, then she paused and handed DI Judd a photograph.

'The final photograph taken, is possibly the photographer's foot, very strange. Why did he take a photo of his foot?' Dr Huntley asked. 'However, if you cast your eyes to the very top of the photograph you can see, what looks like a hand, three knuckles in fact, gripping the photographer's trouser leg. Stranger still, the three knuckles, middle finger, ring finger and little finger of a left hand, have no flesh on them, it's bare bone.' DI Judd looked stunned.

'I have two copies blown up for you to take away,' said the Doctor. 'Also, you may as well take the camera and the film away, I have finished with it, thank you.' The Inspector thanked Dr Huntley, not knowing what to make of it, and left.

The Delany family returned to Ye Olde Elm Tree early evening. The two boys grabbed soft drinks, crisps and headed up to their room to watch television. Mr & Mrs Delany stopped in the bar for a couple of drinks. Some of the conversations they overheard were quite concerning. Man stabbed in the back with a garden fork. Another man died of head wounds. Gardener drowned in the fishpond. Landlord drowned in the cellar.

'Perhaps it's just as well we are checking out tomorrow, for the boys' sake,' said Mr Delany. That night around 2 pm Jack woke up startled. He laid there for several minutes and thought he could hear his name called once more.

'Jack, Jack,' came the voices from the direction of the garden. Jack never ventured to the window this time. He said to himself, this is just a nightmare.

CHAPTER 12 – NEW ARRIVAL

Annie was making breakfast for the Delany family when Mary arrived. Annie apologised to Mary for the mess in the bar. She explained how busy it had been since the news broke.

'If you hoover the snug first Mary, I'll put the Delany family in there, to have their breakfast,' suggested Annie.

The dray arrived with Annie's beer order. Driver Ernie parked next to the cellar hatch. Annie came to meet him with a mug of coffee.

'Horrible business for you Annie,' said Ernie. They chatted a while about the terrible recent occurrences at the pub. Annie explained to Ernie where she would like the beers positioned in the cellar. She might have to tap and vent at least one that day, where she was running quite low.

Mollie telephoned Ye Olde Elm Tree. She can help again in the bar lunchtimes and early evenings, over the weekend. Annie was relieved to hear that.

Annie served breakfast to the Delany Family. Two poached eggs on toast, scrambled eggs for Jack, fruit and cereals for Mrs Delany. Jack just stared at his breakfast, he seemed in a trance.

'What is wrong Jack, are you sickening for something?' asked his mother.

'Can we stop somewhere else tonight? Or go home?' Jack solemnly replied. The breakfast table stopped still, while they digested what Jack had just asked.

'Actually,' answered Mr Delany, 'Your mum and I discussed this last night; we can move on somewhere else, if you like.'

'But where are we going to go?' asked his brother Luke.

'We will find somewhere, don't worry,' replied his father.

Bob Truman turned up with fence posts on his truck. He was determined to concrete as many posts in the ground as he could as the weather forecast for the next two days was heavy storms. Bob had hired a pneumatic drill to help him ease through the work, a Scheppach AB1900 model, with a powerful 1900W motor and 60 joules of impact. Bob drilled down four post holes in no time, when Annie called him into the kitchen for a mug of tea and a bacon sandwich. As they were chatting about recent events there was a rumble, like a slight quake. Bob went back into the garden to see a section of car park wall had fallen, his four post holes filled with sludge. Bob looked at the damage in amazement.

Next to arrive at Ye Olde Elm Tree was totally unexpected; a television news crew. A team of three arrived in a large transit van. A camera man, a reporter with a sound system and a technician. Annie telephoned Reginald Spearing. He advised,

'Let them film what they want, within reason Annie, but try not to conduct a live interview. Insist on a telephone interview if you possibly can. It has worked so far Annie, has it not?' asked Reginald.

'I think so,' Annie replied sheepishly.

Bob Truman reacted quickly. Fortunately, he had some road cones on his truck. He surrounded the sludge-filled holes and tumbled down wall with cones.

The Delany family checked out. Luke really wanted to stay once he had seen the television crew arrive.

'But Mr Delany you are booked in for one more evening?' questioned Annie.

'Yes, that is fine thank you," answered Mr Delany. 'We have some more places we would like try and explore.' Annie offered them a refund, but the Delany family refused to take it. As they departed, Annie looked on bewildered.

Next to arrive was the photographer from the Star News.

'Good morning Mrs Baines, I am the Star News photographer, Eamon Fuller. I believe you have agreed with Godfrey Wallace from our paper, that I could take a few photographs of the pub itself, and the location of the recent accident and where the murder took place.'

The television crew heard this and were ambitiously interested too. What a paradoxical situation thought Annie, as she showed both the photographer and the crew the corner of the pub where the lean-to once stood, the garden shed where the garden fork came from, finally the spot where Mary and Annie found Gresham's body. Unfortunately, the police still had custody of the garden fork. Bob Truman watched all this in awe. Eamon Fuller was quite happy, he wandered around the garden and inside the pub, clicking away to his heart's content. The film crew camera man was too, not the reporter though; Annie insisted on a telephone interview and disappeared back inside the pub.

Within half an hour of the television crew arriving at Ye Olde Elm Tree, a second crew arrived from a competitive TV channel. A crew of four this time. Annie had to point out the locations to another camera man. This is an insane situation, she thought.

Annie telephoned Charles Braithwaite to warn him that two television teams had turned up at Ye Olde Elm Tree, plus the Star News were planning a feature. Charles hung up and thought, great publicity, he was quite excited.

Annie took a telephone call from Edgar in New Zealand. Annie was totally surprised to hear from him. Edgar offered to come and stop with Annie. He could book a direct flight from Auckland, New Zealand to the UK, hire a car and be with Annie by Tuesday morning.

'That would be lovely,' answered Annie. She had a lot of time for Edgar; he reminded Annie of her late husband Bert.

The next telephone call was a gentleman looking for a room for the night, that night. Plenty of room thought Annie, especially as the Delany family have checked out. Annie confirmed a room was available and gave him a price. She asked him for his name and contact details.

'Toby Devons is the name,' the caller replied and gave Annie a mobile telephone number. Annie put the phone down and shuddered; it was the name.

Nightmares at Ye Olde Elm Tree

The Star News photographer and the television film crews left just before opening time. Annie was relieved. It was then, she saw a police car draw up in the car park. It was DI Judd. Annie ushered the inspector into the snug, while Mollie kept the customers in the main bar happy. DI Judd declined refreshment, that was never a good start to the discussion in Annie's judgement. The inspector reached into her briefcase and pulled out an enlarged photograph. She handed it to Annie.

'Why have you given me a photo of someone's foot?' asked Annie.

DI Judd explained, 'This was the last photograph taken in the camera found in your garden. If you look carefully at the top of the picture, you see three knuckles of a left hand, gripping the person's trouser leg.'

'If you say so,' replied Annie sarcastically.

'Yes, we do say so,' replied the Inspector, 'How do you explain that those three knuckles appear to have no flesh on them?'

'I can't,' exclaimed Annie, 'Trick photography.' Annie smirked and handed the photograph back to DI Judd.

'We are about to start a full-scale search for the photographer, Gordon McLarty. This may involve more excavation on your property Annie, in the vicinity where the camera was found,' declared the Inspector. 'Good day Annie, we will be in touch,' said DI Judd. She popped the photograph back into her briefcase and returned to her car. Annie shook her head in disbelief.

That lunchtime was busy, so many faces asking questions, that Annie had never laid eyes on before. The evening was similar although there were several locals in for early doors. Farmer Forde, Granville, Monica, Desmond People, and his girlfriend Alice. At around 8 pm Jules Jameson and Norm Prince came in. Jules explained how they will start the card school once more on a Tuesday evening, albeit just the three players this time. Jules wanted to personally apologise to Annie about saying some condemning things about her and the lean-to. He had time to think about it and had reached a conclusion, that it was a freakish accident. Annie thanked him, took guts to say that she thought.

Annie looked at the clock at 9.30 wondering where Mr Devons was, who had booked a room at the last minute. Soon afterwards, a 1970's Jeep rolled up into Ye Olde Elm Tree car park. Toby Devons did not bother to lock the vehicle. On entering the bar, he inspected the range of beers that Annie had on offer.

'I think I will try the strongest ale you have, 5.6% ABV, that will do for me,' said Toby. Mollie poured his pint, Annie watched dubiously.

'Mr Devons?' asked Annie; that turned a few heads.

'Yes, Toby Devons is the name. I believe you have a room for me this evening?' he replied. Most people that stay at Ye Olde Elm Tree arrive with small suitcases and a bag or two, Toby Devons just had a duffel bag slung across his shoulder. His appearance was generally scruffy, muddy boots, corduroy trousers, tweed jacket, soiled looking shirt and a flat cap. He had long grey hair protruding from his cap and a wispy grey beard.

'Would you like to see your room Mr Devons?' asked Annie. 'I have put you on the top floor with nice views, weather permitting, overlooking the garden and local hillside.'

'No thanks, I'll retire soon enough, once I have sunk a few more of your strongest ales,' sneered Toby. It was not long before Toby went outside to smoke a cigarette. It was quite a still night, half moon, appearing intermittently behind fast moving clouds. He ventured around the side of the pub and peered into the car park. A few drags on his cigarette and he proceeded to the rear of the pub; he walked toward the corner of the building, where Garrett Devons' accident happened. Suddenly, there was an extremely strong gust of wind. Toby had to grab his cap to keep it on his head. He swore, stubbed out his cigarette and went back into the pub.

Mollie left around 10.30 pm, she had promised some early morning dog walking, next morning. The pub had started to clear out a little. Toby Devons started to ask Annie questions about the accident and the garden fork murder. Annie felt uncomfortable. He seemed to know a lot of detail.

'You are talking as if you know the two men involved,' suggested Annie.

'Yes, I do,' he replied, 'They were my cousins.' Annie dropped a glass, it smashed into several pieces.

After Annie had cleared up the mess, Toby Devons ordered another pint and went outside for another cigarette. There was a small group of teenagers in the bar playing darts; it looked as if they were about to leave the pub, so while Toby was outside, Annie offered to treat them to one final drink at closing time should they stay. She did not want to be left alone with Toby Devons.

Closing time arrived soon enough. Annie escorted Toby to his room. She stood back as he entered the room. He took a long look around the room, looked back at Annie, stared at her and said,

'Goodnight,' and pushed the door shut.

'Goodnight,' murmured Annie under her breath. There was more clearing up to do down in the bar, but Annie went straight to her room, her hands were clammy, her throat was dry. Fortunately, Annie had a latch on her bedroom door, she latched the door and went straight to bed. Annie was scared and afraid of her new guest.

CHAPTER 13 – THE CALLING

It took Toby Devons quite a while to drop off to sleep. He was contemplating how to settle a score with Annie. He kept thinking of the telephone conversation he had with his cousin Gresham, the day before he died. Gresham was convinced it was Annie's neglect on the property that got Garrett killed, and now Gresham had been killed, murdered. Toby did eventually drop off to sleep, but not for long. In the early hours of the morning there were three very loud bangs on his bedroom door.

'What the hell,' he woke up startled. It happened again, three very loud bangs on his door. 'Who is it?' shouted Toby. Silence.

He scrambled out of bed, quickly put some trousers on, unlatched his door and flung it open. There was no one there! Toby looked along the corridor both ways; he could not see anything; it was too dark. It had to be that evil landlady he thought. He scrambled across his bed and reached for his mobile phone, he switched the torch on and ventured into the corridor, shone the torch in both directions, nothing there. Toby decided to go down a flight of stairs and sort that landlady out!

'Mrs Baines,' he yelled, 'What do you think you are playing at?' That call woke up Annie. Toby called out once more, 'Mrs Baines, where are you?' He was not sure which was Annie's bedroom. It was then he noticed a sign on one of the doors, 'Annie's Room,' he stopped outside it. Annie put on her dressing gown and went to the door. I must not unlatch the door she thought.

Annie called out, 'What is wrong Mr Devons?'

'You banged on my bedroom door loudly, six times altogether, why? What are you playing at woman, in the middle of the night?' yelled an angry Toby Devons.

Annie did not like his tone! 'I did nothing of the sort,' Annie was trembling. 'Now please go back to bed or I will call the police.' She thought, how am I going to do that? Annie never had a telephone in her bedroom and she certainly was not going to open her bedroom door.

'Are you saying you didn't bang my door? Then who did?' Toby asked; he had lowered his tone slightly.

'Heaven knows,' said Annie, 'Are you sure you weren't hearing things? Now please go back to bed, lets discuss this in the morning.' Reluctantly Toby turned around, walked along the corridor and climbed the stairs to his bedroom.

Mary arrived at Ye Olde Elm Tree as punctual as ever. Annie never slept well that night; she was already up and dressed when Mary arrived. Annie blurted out to Mary what had happened last night and who her guest was.

'I would call the police, Annie. This is a very strange predicament you have here,' advised Mary.

Charles Braithwaite was up early on this Sunday morning. He helped himself to a hearty breakfast, an hour with the national paper he thought, then he would start preparing for his board meeting presentation next morning.

Annie's brother-in-law Edgar had boarded the aeroplane from Auckland, New Zealand. I will soon be with Annie, he thought. Just two days, three calendar days, to travel the entire distance.

Annie telephoned Mollie and invited her to stop the evening at Ye Olde Elm Tree after her shift on the bar that evening. Annie explained that she might take a few hours off and relax. That was fine with Mollie.

Mary walked into the kitchen. Toby Devons had ventured downstairs for breakfast. Annie gave a sigh and went to greet him. Toby ordered a full English breakfast. After he had eaten his breakfast, Annie went to clear his plates away. 'Will there be anything else Mr Devons?' asked Annie.

'Yes, there is actually,' Toby replied in a soft tone. 'I have two wreaths in the back of my jeep, one for Garrett and one for Gresham. I would like to lay them on the exact spots, where they were killed.' Annie's face drained of colour.

'Actually Mr. Devons, I was going to ask you to leave and not stop the night, after last night's episode.'

The old cow thought Toby.

'Mrs Baines, surely you don't begrudge me the opportunity to pay respects to my two cousins?' Toby said cunningly. 'What if some of your locals found out that you showed no remorse to a close relative of two brothers who died tragically at your public house.'

'Give me half an hour to tidy up the kitchen, and I'll show you those locations,' said Annie, who was trembling with anger as she walked back into the kitchen.

Detective Inspector Judd returned a call to reporter Nick Fitzsimons. 'Hello Mr Fitzsimons, I'd like to speak to you regarding your friend Gordon McLarty, the photographer,' said the Inspector.

'Ah, glad you called Inspector,' replied Nick, 'This is really weird, Gordon has just disappeared, it's not like him, I feel something is wrong, I know it is. His phone seems out of action, it's preternatural.'

DI Judd asked the reporter for Mr McLarty's mobile phone number so she could organise a trace on it. She also questioned him on any background he could shed, of Gordon McLarty, friends, family? Nick explained that Gordon had moved down from Glasgow approximately three years ago, after splitting up with his wife Moira.

'Do you have an address for Gordon McLarty and possibly Moira McLarty by any chance?' asked the Inspector.

'Sorry inspector, I only have Gordons address, I have been around to his apartment twice, but he's not been there. His ex-wife changed her name back to her maiden name after their marriage split. I have no idea what her maiden name was, Gordon never said.' Nick gave DI Judd Gordon's address. I can see this is not going to be straight forward, she thought.

Annie met Toby Devons at the breakfast table to show him the two locations. They left the pub through the front door, and walked around the side of the pub. Annie glanced at Toby's jeep, plastered in mud. His tatty vehicle matched Toby Devons' tatty appearance, she thought. They reached the back corner of the building where the lean-to once stood.

'This is where Garrett had his accident,' Annie said quietly.

Toby suddenly reflected on the previous evening; that was the exact spot where a strong gust of wind nearly took his hat off. Must be a sign he thought. Annie then led Toby toward the garden shed. She stopped just short.

'This is where my cleaner Mary found Gresham,' said Annie.

'Cleaner found him?' questioned Toby.

'It was my dog that actually discovered your cousin, my cleaner Mary had let the dog out into the garden, I was still upstairs.' Annie shut up quickly, she felt she had said too much already.

'If it is ok with you Mrs Baines, I will now lay wreaths in those two places,' said Toby.

'Very well,' confirmed Annie, who walked back into the pub via the back door. Toby Devons returned to his vehicle and opened the back door. His eyes set on the two wreaths. His eyes then became glued; in the back of his jeep was an axe wrapped in a muslin cloth stockinette.

DI Judd had returned to her office. The trace on Gordon McLarty's mobile phone proved negative. The last cell site recorded was in the vicinity of the public house Ye Olde Elm Tree. The telephone operator reported that there was no longer a cellular signal existing. The Inspector was stunned with this finding. She contacted the City of Glasgow Police Department. She spoke to DI Ashleigh McGregor and explained the situation of the possible missing person of Gordon McLarty and the need to trace his ex-wife Moira. She added that Moira had changed her name by deed poll, to her maiden name. DI McGregor promised to investigate it further for her.

Toby Devons laid the two wreaths down in the areas where his cousins' bodies were found. He took a cast iron garden seat from the back wall of the pub and placed it in the garden, next to the wreath laid for Gresham. He sat on the seat and lit a cigarette. Annie could see this from her kitchen window; how audacious of him she thought. Her hostility for Toby Devons was growing. As Toby sat and pondered on how to get even with the landlady, he was reflecting on a film he watched in the early 1980's, The Shining. Jack Nicholson played a character with a degree of lunacy, in Jack Torrance. One scene came to mind, where he axed through a door to try and reach his wife in the film, Wendy. Toby had an axe in his jeep. He could chop his way through the landlady's bedroom door! That would scare her he thought, that would be fun. He smoked another cigarette, walked to his vehicle, took the muslin cloth from the jeep and smuggled it upstairs into his bedroom.

Annie received a telephone call from one of the producers of the TV company that had filmed at Ye Olde Elm Tree the previous day. Annie asked the caller to hold, while she ran upstairs to her living room, to fetch her notes. She then picked up the receiver in the upstairs room; she did not want Toby Devons to hear any of the conversation with the TV company. After the call, Annie went back down to the bar and came face to face with Toby Devons, which startled her.

'Did I make you jump?' said Toby gleefully, 'I have decided to pay Garrett and Gresham's parents a visit. Their grief must be unbearable.'

Annie tried so hard not to react to his sarcasm. She watched him drive off in his jeep and thought now was her chance, she telephoned Detective Inspector Judd. Annie explained how Toby Devons had introduced himself, how he was stopping at Ye Olde Elm Tree for two nights, the incident in the middle of the night, and the episode with the wreaths in the garden. She also told the inspector how he drinks heavily and how scared she is of him! DI Judd promised to call in to Ye Olde Elm Tree that evening, to make his acquaintance.

By the lunchtime, the stormy weather predicted had arrived. Despite the storm, the pub was busy with onlookers, as well as locals. Annie was glad of Mollie's help with the bar.

The evening trade was not quite so busy. Annie had kept to her promise and had sloped off upstairs for a few hours relaxation and to watch television. Toby Devons arrived back at Ye Olde Elm Tree just before 7.30 pm. He wasted no time in ordering a pint of the strongest ale available. An hour later, DI Judd arrived at Ye Olde Elm Tree. Mollie pointed out Toby Devons to the inspector; he was sat in the corner of the bar with his pint, playing games on his mobile phone. It kept him amused, so he did not see the detective enter the bar.

'Mind if I join you a moment?' asked DI Judd. Toby's face showed no emotion.

'Please yourself,' he replied. The inspector thought that was a confident, but unnecessary response.

'I was told you are a cousin of the Devons' brothers, come to pay your respects,' indicated DI Judd. 'I am one of the leading investigators into your cousins' deaths.'

'Well you don't have to look any further,' barked Toby. 'The murderer is sitting upstairs watching television.' DI Judd was suddenly aware of Toby's intense hostility toward Annie Baines.

'Thank you for your opinion, Mr Devons,' replied the Inspector. 'Mrs Baines has been helping us with our enquiries. Will you be staying at Ye Olde Elm Tree, or locally, much longer Mr Devons?' she asked.

'Depends. I can stay as long as I like,' he replied.

'Depends on what, Mr Devons?' enquired the Inspector.

'I am here to mourn the loss of my cousins, so why shouldn't I stay as long as I want?' he questioned the officer.

She paused and answered, 'That may not be in everybody's best interests.' DI Judd gave Toby a scornful look and bid him farewell and to have a nice evening. The inspector chose not to bother Annie Baines and left Ye Old Elm Tree. Toby finished off his pint, approached the bar and ordered another pint. He was convinced that old cow of a landlady was responsible for that intrusion.

Toby Devons went to bed after closing time. He was curious why barmaid Mollie was clearing up rather than the landlady. He laid on his bed waiting for a suitable time to play some tricks on his host. He was not aware Mollie was staying at the pub that night. He nodded off. Annie and Mollie hugged each other goodnight; Annie was so relieved on someone else sleeping at Ye Olde Elm Tree that night. In the early hours of the morning the rain was lashing against Toby's bedroom window. It woke Toby. Shit he thought, what time is it? He grabbed for his mobile phone it was 2.30 am. He needed to gather his thoughts together. Had he lost the opportunity to scare the landlady. He was conscious the axe would now, not be a good idea, following the visit of the police officer. What else could he do? It was then he thought he heard his name called.

'Toby, Toby.' It came from the direction of the garden. The rain was still crashing down on his bedroom window, so he may have been hearing things. It came again,

'Toby, Toby.' He pushed the bed clothes back and went to the window opening it wide.

'Toby, Toby.' The voices seemed to be coming from directly below him, perhaps against the pub wall. Toby leaned further out of the window, trying to see where the voices were coming from. The rain was lashing him in the face. Then, it was as if someone, something, had grabbed his legs to push him out of the window. With his left hand he managed to grab hold of the window frame to stop him from falling. Then came excruciating pain, and Toby let out a scream. It was as if something very sharp had cut into his wrist, like an axe. Toby fell twenty feet, to his death.

CHAPTER 14 – FRONT PAGE NEWS

Annie had a restless night; she could not get out of her head what happened the night before. She half expected a repeat performance; she was relieved however the night was incident free. Mollie was first up. She was accustomed to getting up early to walk her dogs. Mollie went downstairs to the kitchen to make a cup of tea. Chester was very restless.

What's got into you this morning Chester?' asked Mollie as she ruffled his fur. Mollie opened the back door for Chester and let out a scream. Toby Devons' body was laid on the path close to the pub wall. There was a lot of blood from a head wound; he looked dead. Annie heard her scream and quickly came downstairs.

'T-toby Devons' body is outside the back door,' stuttered Mollie. Annie was almost afraid to look. Clutching Mollie by the arm, Annie stood over the dead body. Mollie was shaking and sobbing; she had never seen anything quite so horrible before. Annie called Chester back into the pub and shut the back door. Annie offered Mollie comfort with a strong cup of tea. Annie reached for the telephone and called Detective Inspector Judd's mobile; it was on answer phone.

'Hello Inspector Judd, this is Annie Baines at Ye Olde Elm Tree, I'm afraid there has been a terrible accident, can you call me please?' Annie's voice was quivering.

At 8.30 Annie was at the pub's front door waiting for Mary to arrive. Mary wound down her car window. This was unexpected, Mary thought, must be something wrong.

'Mary, don't use the back door this morning, one of our customers has had an accident, we think he might be dead.' Mary looked horrified.

'Another death,' exclaimed Mary, 'Oh my goodness.' She then reached over onto her back seat and produced a copy of the Star News newspaper. Annie and Ye Olde Elm Tree was front page news.

The three ladies sat in the kitchen not knowing what to say. Annie studied the newspaper article; there were many of Annie's quotes from her telephone interview. There were four photographs; one of Annie with her dog Chester, another of the front view of the pub, a photograph of the spot where the lean-to once stood; and oddly, a photograph of the old elm tree, at the bottom of the garden. Annie realised later that the article closed with the tragic death of her husband Bert in the cellar, and how Bert had renamed the pub from the King's Arms. Mollie gave Annie a big hug and left to go dog walking; she was not looking forward to it after such torrential rain last night.

The pub phone rang, it was DI Judd. The inspector was in her police vehicle clutching a copy of the Star News. Annie broke the news to the officer, on what had happened to Toby Devons. DI Judd was astounded. She wasted no time in calling Detective Chief Superintendent Raj Thackeray with the alarming news.

Annie opened the back door, this time with Mary present. They stood over the body. Annie was still stunned and dismayed at what had happened.

'He must have fallen from quite a height,' derived Mary, 'Was he on the top floor?' Annie nodded. They both stared up at a wide-open window on the second floor.

'Mary will you come up to his bedroom with me?' Annie asked, 'I haven't been up to his room yet.' The two ladies climbed the two flights of stairs. Annie went to open the bedroom door; it was latched from the inside.

Pandemonium broke out at Ye Olde Elm Tree in the following half hour period. DI Judd, DCS Thackeray and DS Roach all arrived in separate vehicles. Two forensic vehicles and the EMS arrived, Emergency Medical Services, it would be their responsibility to make sure that the risk of harm was mitigated. Police contractor George Pullman arrived, with his truck with a mini digger loaded. Bob Truman also arrived to start work again on the fence posts. The police turned Bob away; he was asked to return on a different day. Bob had to find out what had happened. He parked his van in the nearby layby and rang Annie from his mobile phone. Afterwards Annie put the phone down on Bob and thought this is not going to be a normal Monday morning, no cellar work and pipe cleaning for her today. The police had two options to gain entry to the latched bedroom; climb through the open bedroom window, Ye Olde Elm Tree, apparently had a pair of aluminium ladders, or simply break down the door. The EMS would not allow the ladder option, so DI Judd put a call into the station for an enforcer.

Annie took a call from the television company. Ye Olde Elm Tree was to feature on their 1 pm news bulletin. The broadcaster was unaware of the Toby Devons casualty. Annie thought she was going to need more help than just

Mollie at this rate. She in-turn telephoned Charles Braithwaite, to inform him of the television broadcast.

Annie watched as a police constable battered the door open. The superintendent and inspector entered the room first. They saw an unmade bed, a pile of clothes and a duffle bag on a chair, then embedded into the window's wooden sill was an axe. Annie was stood behind them in the corridor, horrified. He had an axe in his room, what was he going to do with an axe? She turned and walked down the flight of stairs; she had to go and sit down. A forensic officer removed the axe and picked up the muslin cloth which they assumed Toby Devons may have used, to hide the axe.

Charles Braithwaite looked his usual dapper self for his presentation to the board of directors. He presented some history first, of Ye Olde Elm Tree since Albert and Annie Baines invested in the lease ten years previously. Charles presented steady growth in sales revenue and emphasised the majority being wet sales. He then projected an estimate for future growth in the present year. He admitted that Annie Baines had been helping the police with their enquiries, but there was no incriminating evidence on Mrs Baines, so she continues to trade, and trade well. He produced a Star News newspaper with a front-page account at Ye Olde Elm Tree. Then came his sucker punch, the television broadcast company would be showing a news feature on Ye Olde Elm Tree, that very day. Charles offered his assurance to the directors that he would be overseeing daily events at Ye Olde Elm Tree until the speculation and public interest had died down. The board sanctioned his commitment. They also decided to break for lunch at 12.45 pm in time to watch the TV bulletin.

DCS Thackeray and DI Judd interviewed Annie extensively in the snug at Ye Olde Elm Tree. She told them the whole story from when Toby Devons first arrived. Fortunately for Annie, DI Judd had experienced Toby Devons' hostility the night before. Annie put in a call to Mollie, asking her to return to Ye Olde Elm Tree, as the two officers wanted to speak to Mollie next. There were no arrests or accusations made.

Mollie covered the lunchtime shift on the bar so that Annie could watch the television report at 1 pm. Afterwards Annie thought the report was quite damning, it did not reflect well on her.

The EMS ambulance took the body away to the forensic laboratory for further examination. George was given the all-clear to unload his mini digger. DS Roach was assigned to oversee the excavation. Reporter Nick Fitzsimons turned up at Ye Olde Elm Tree. Nick was keen to learn if there had been any progress in trying to locate missing Gordon McLarty. DS Roach explained that unforeseen circumstances had held them up starting the excavation work, however they were about to commence. The sergeant never told Nick Fitzsimons what exactly had held them up. Nick questioned the sergeant,

'Why are you digging using a JCB, officer? Do you think Gordon's body was buried?'

DS Roach replied, 'It's a formality, we have dug at this site before for missing persons, just a formality.' Nick thought his explanation was bizarre.

Annie looked in the pub diary; two families were booked in for the following weekend. A Hooper family and a Woodhall family, all four rooms fully booked. Annie called Bob Truman; could he come over to Ye Olde Elm Tree to measure up for a new bedroom door and latch.

DI Judd took a call from DI McGregor, City of Glasgow Police Department. Moira McLarty had been located. She had changed her surname via Deed Poll to Bannerman. DI McGregor had personally called on Moira to investigate the whereabouts of Gordon McLarty. His ex-wife had only seen him once since the marriage had split up three years previous, when Gordon moved to England. The only contact she had was a child maintenance standing order each month. DI Judd thanked DI McGregor for her help. Another brick wall, thought DI Judd. The inspector then proceeded to make two calls that she was hoping she did not have to make, to the ICMP, International Commission on Missing Persons, and the NCIC, National Crime Information Centre, to inform them of Gordon McLarty.

The first dig proved unsuccessful where DS Roach had indicated, which was where he had lifted the camera from. They tried a second dig slightly further down the garden, toward the old elm tree. Twenty minutes into the second excavation, the digger struck something. George turned off the engine. DS Roach rushed to the location.

'It looks like some kind of wooden box, quite rotten, been in the ground a few years,' he called to George. George went in pursuit of a spade from his truck. Very carefully he started to dig around the box. It appeared larger than at first. George went to scrape some mud off the top of it, when part of it collapsed, exposing an arm and a hand, of a skeleton.

CHAPTER 15 – CALL IN THE EXPERTISE

Detective Sergeant Roach called Detective Inspector Judd on his mobile phone. DI Judd had returned to the station and had the laborious task of reporting the accidental death of Toby Devons. The sergeant explained to the inspector what they had discovered, with the skeleton, at Ye Olde Elm Tree.

'You must stop the dig Sergeant,' instructed DI Judd. 'With human remains, we will have to call in our Anthropologist's expertise. I came across something similar several years ago, the Anthropologist can call on a team of Archaeologists to join the excavation, and they will have to apply for a permit to excavate the site further. We will need to cover over the site securely for this evening.'

'But surely Guv,' replied DS Roach.

'No buts, Sergeant, make sure George has a tarpaulin that can be fastened down dependably. We cannot afford any more accidents at Ye Olde Elm Tree.' DS Roach informed George what had to be done next.

'I can bring a tarpaulin over in the morning, Sergeant. That's a shame we can't carry on,' said George.

'Sorry George we have to secure the area before we go home tonight,' informed the Sergeant. George reluctantly returned to his truck and drove off to his local yard.

DS Roach informed Annie of their findings and that an Anthropologist would be called upon to manage the excavation further, as they had discovered human remains. This is like one big nightmare, Annie thought! DS Roach explained how they would have to make the site safe and secure. Afterwards Annie phoned Bob Truman,

'Can you come back tomorrow Bob?' said Annie, 'The police are about to finish up here.' Bob agreed to pick up the door and be over first thing. Annie never explained to Bob what the police had discovered, she was too mentally exhausted.

Ye Olde Elm Tree was headlines in all the morning papers, next morning, with the breaking news of Toby Devons' death, a third family member to be killed in a matter of weeks at this quintessential old English public house. The police had put out a statement that suicide was suspected. The locked bedroom door from the inside, was proving to be a mystery. The axe mark, on Toby Devons' wrist, was even a bigger mystery, for the police department. The TV broadcast unit decided not to return to Ye Olde Elm Tree for their reporting of the Toby Devons' death, but focused on the remaining Devons family, instead.

Charles Braithwaite sat down for breakfast, smoked kippers, and scrambled eggs; he was really looking forward to it. His morning was planned to drive to Ye Olde Elm Tree, for his first sales call. Charles opened his newspaper and saw the headlines, 'THIRD RELATIVE KILLED AT YE OLDE ELM TREE.' He read the entire report, then cast the newspaper aside. Charles informed his wife, what he has just read.

'Better eat your breakfast dear, you may have a busy day ahead,' replied his wife.

Nick Fitzsimons took a telephone call from a colleague informing him of the Toby Devons' accident. So that is why the dig for Gordon was interrupted, he thought, how interesting. He promised himself, another visit to Ye Olde Elm Tree, later that day.

Nightmares at Ye Olde Elm Tree

Mollie lived with her parents in the local village, in a small terraced house. She was friends with her next-door neighbour, Jimmy, aged nineteen, left school at sixteen. In that time, he had held half a dozen jobs. Mollie mentioned to Jimmy about helping on the bar at Ye Olde Elm Tree.

'I would love to work there,' was Jimmy's response, 'I might actually see a real murder!' Nice lad thought Mollie, but so immature.

Charles Braithwaite arrived at Ye Olde Elm Tree during the lunchtime trading; it was busy with tourists. Charles said hello to Annie and noticed young Jimmy on the bar.

'Who's he?' asked Charles.

'A friend of Mollie's' answered Annie, 'He is a bit green behind the ears but a helping pair of hands. How was your board meeting?' asked Annie.

'Fine,' replied Charles, 'I put a positive spin on how trade was going well here, the board were happy. What happened with Toby Devons?' he asked.

'The idiot threw himself out of the top bedroom window,' stated Annie. 'He was as nutty as a fruitcake! He even had an axe in his bedroom! A bloody axe!' divulged Annie. Charles looked perplexed.

It was Tuesday afternoon. A hire car turned into the car park at Ye Olde Elm Tree. it was Annie's brother-in-law Edgar. He was astounded, he hardly had room to park his car, the car park was so full. He lifted the boot of the car, and took out his suitcase. Annie came to greet him. They hugged for a good minute. Annie had to explain though, Edgar only had a room until Friday, then he would have to sleep on the couch for a few days, Ye Olde Elm Tree was fully booked for the weekend.

That evening the card school met, despite there being only three players. Edgar offered to join in, to make up a fourth player. The school were delighted; they taught Edgar how to play chase the lady.

Wednesday morning, Bob Truman turned up with a new door for the bedroom, and fence posts to try once more. Happy days, thought Bob.

At the police station, DI Judd had organised a meeting with her department to include, Dr Cynthia Bell an Anthropologist, who would be taking responsibility for recovering the human artefact at Ye Olde Elm Tree, and an Archaeologist, Dr David Donnelly, who would be assisting Dr Bell. Dr Donnelly spoke first to the team; his responsibility was to determine clues, as to the past of the artefact.

'It is rather like detective work except we are more story tellers, our evidence does not have to stand up in court.' claimed Dr Donnelly. The audience laughed at the Archaeologist's synopsis.

Dr Bell went on to explain her responsibilities with the excavation. She explained that in a normal archaeological dig all the evidence should be collected and documented, such as ground surface, plants, insects, objects such as clothing, weapons, or human remains. She told the team that she accepted this was not a normal archaeological excavation, but it was essential to record every single stage of the operation. This is going to be a long drawn out enquiry, thought DI Judd.

Wednesday evening at Ye Old Elm Tree, the darts team were at home to the King and Queen pub from the local village. This was to be a big turn-out, there were a lot of supporters from the village. The away side offered a team of up to ten players, Ye Olde Elm Tree had seven. Edgar stepped forward and made eight. Much to the delight of the home team, Edgar won his game. It was the first time Annie had laughed in a long time.

With the permit in place, the process accelerated by the police department, the professional excavation started on the Thursday, with Dr Bell, and Dr Donnelly only. DS Roach was again assigned to oversee the work. This is like watching paint dry, thought the DS. He chose to check on the team periodically. On one occasion, reporter Nick Fitzsimons turned up at Ye Olde Elm Tree. The sergeant had to explain to Nick, that this was now an archaeological excavation.

'How is that going to find Gordon McLarty?' Nick bellowed.

'It may not,' replied the Sergeant, 'We have reported your missing friend Mr McLarty to the correct authorities.' Nick was not happy with the explanation he received; he wanted to make trouble for the police department over this, but was not sure how he could.

By the end of the afternoon the excavation had exposed a coffin. The lid was extremely rotten. The team decided to secure the site and attempt to remove the coffin lid next morning. DS Roach phoned the status of the dig through to DI Judd.

'A coffin,' said the Inspector with a pause, 'I wonder who, could possibly be in it?'

Thursday there was no excavation due to heavy rain. In the evening it was quiz night at Ye Olde Elm Tree. Alfie Richardson, who organises the evening was delighted, it was a full house. Edgar was invited onto the card school quiz team. Annie was delighted for Edgar, as his team had won the quiz.

On the Friday, Bob Truman arrived to fit the fence panels and side gate. The Archaeologists team were quite relieved; this should reduce the number of gawkers at the site, they both agreed. The two families booked in for the weekend both arrived at Ye Olde Elm Tree, one hour apart. Annie had to explain to both families why a section of the car park was sectioned off, with a police presence.

'It is an archaeological excavation,' explained Annie.

'Oh! How interesting,' said Mrs Hooper. Annie had booked the Hooper family on the top floor. The Woodhall family were also extremely interested in what was going on.

'Can we take photographs?' asked Mrs Woodhall.

'Not sure if that will be possible,' answered Annie, with a wry smile. Edgar was resigned to sleeping on the couch for the weekend.

At the close of Friday's excavation, the team had exposed the full-length coffin, rotted to such an extent that they believed it would not survive any upheaval. They had successfully removed the lid; inside, they deduced, was a middle-aged woman, just over five feet in height; some bones had separated from the main body. The team agreed to cover over the site for the weekend, then carefully lift the artefacts on Monday for further examination back in the laboratory.

The Hooper children, Rebecca 13, Rachel 11, went to bed that evening quite excited about this long weekend away. The dig at the back of the pub was in full view from their bedroom window. The couple carrying out the exhumation had covered it completely with tarpaulin, so sadly there was not very much to see. They giggled and chatted for a good hour before they fell off to sleep. It was somewhere between 2 and 3 am in the morning, that Rachel got out of bed and went to her bedroom window. It was quite dark outside, she struggled to see anything. Her eyes were fixed in the direction of the excavation. She stared at something there, it looked like a shadow, a silhouette standing over the tarpaulin. She peered at it for quite a while. The shadow stood motionless, perfectly still, looking down toward the ground. Rachel thought no more about it, rubbed her eyes and went back to bed.

CHAPTER 16 – THE NIGHT CALL

Early Saturday morning, Detective Sergeant Roach was down at the station writing his report for the Detective Chief Superintendent, on the professional excavation at Ye Olde Elm Tree. Detective Inspector Judd would oversee the report, before it made its way into the 'Supers' office. Such a lot of paperwork, thought DI Judd. She happened to be dealing with an unexpected new challenge. The family solicitor for sales manager, Geoff Foreman, one of the three missing men, had emailed the Inspector's office, having learnt of the excavation to try and find the missing salesmen and their vehicle at Ye Olde Elm Tree. I am not sure how to answer this, thought the detective.

Charles Braithwaite had popped into his office on Saturday morning. He started by approving another emergency order for beer from Ye Olde Elm Tree. His monthly sales report was available. The first thing he looked for was the sales figure for Ye Olde Elm Tree. Wet sales up 35 percent; Charles was pleased. His sales area had a total of over thirty hotels and public houses. He read down the list, fifteen had negative growth that month; that is high thought Charles, nearly half. He would need to understand the reasons behind the short-fall, or he is likely to receive another call from his board of directors.

DS Roach finished his report on the excavation. Dr Bell had provided him with a list of facts to include in the report. He telephoned reporter Nick Fitzsimons, to inform him that a small team, including forensic officers, were about to search Gordon McLarty's apartment, having received the necessary search warrant. Nick asked to tag along; he was told he could, but he would not be allowed to enter the premises during the search.

Annie had a busy morning cooking breakfasts for eight customers, fortunately Mary was there to help. Afterwards she sat down and had breakfast with Edgar. Her brother-in-law asked her outright,

'Why do you carry on with this old pub Annie? Why don't you retire?'

Annie gave Edgar an honest answer, 'I have nothing else, this is my life, my income, my home.' She replied earnestly.

'But Annie the upkeep, the worry, with no Bert to help you manage the business anymore, it must be such a strain? And now you have three deaths, four missing persons, you have been arrested, customers checking out before their time, hordes of nosy tourists, rooms fully booked for weekends ahead. I worry this lifestyle will catch up with you sooner, or later.' Edgar's searching summary was sincere.

'Where would I go Edgar?' Annie asked. 'I do not have another home to go to, or income to live off, I don't have any plans in place.'

Edgar reached out and clasped Annie's hands. 'Come back with me to New Zealand,' suggested Edgar. 'I have a large property, I am self-sufficient, quite lonely since Agatha died which is twelve years ago now. No strings attached. I could offer you the west wing of the house to live in. Please give it some thought Annie. It could be a fresh start for you, leaving all this crazy business behind you.' Annie looked quite shocked and solemnly surprised. She was not expecting that innuendo from Edgar.

'I will certainly consider your offer Edgar. Thank you for your very kind proposal,' responded Annie.

Annie did think about Edgar's offer for most of the day, it took her mind off the recent deaths temporarily. Leaving her sister Nancy back home would be a real wrench though.

The Saturday lunchtime trade was busy again. Annie had both Mollie and Jimmy to help her. Mollie was quick to point out that an elderly couple that had just entered Ye Olde Elm Tree was Garrett and Gresham's parents. They happened to be accompanied by another relative, another cousin.

'How do you know?' asked Annie.

'I recognise them from the TV report yesterday, they were all interviewed.' Annie suddenly felt quite uncomfortable, almost nauseated.

A team of four police and forensic officers arrived at Gordon McLarty's apartment. They spent over an hour going through his personal belongings and searching his property for clues on why he might have disappeared. Afterwards, DS Roach approached Nick Fitzsimons, who was sat outside in his car.

'We have searched extensively Mr Fitzsimons, there is no indication whatsoever on why Mr McLarty has gone missing, no clues from inside his apartment,' the Sergeant informed him. This was not what Nick Fitzsimons wanted to hear.

The Hooper family had enjoyed the day at the local lake. It was a shame, but it was not the best of weather and Mr

Hooper insisted on a vigorous hillside walk. They returned to Ye Olde Elm Tree and met up with the Woodhall family in the bar. The two families had never met before but agreed to go out together, in search for somewhere to have dinner. The conversation over dinner was at times mercurial. The newspaper headlines, the archaeological excavation, they all agreed they were stopping at the right place, at the right time.

In the early hours of the morning, the Hooper family, Woodhall family, Annie, and Edgar on the couch, were all fast asleep. The night was quite still, a mist in the form of a drizzle was slowly sweeping over the hillside. Rachel heard her name called.

'Rachel, Rachel,' it was like a chant. When Rachel was much younger, she was renowned for sleep walking. Her mother would fix a child gate at her bedroom door, to prevent her. Rachel slowly left her bed, opened her bedroom door, and walked unhurriedly down two flights of stairs. Not a soul heard her. It was as if she was entranced. It was as if she knew exactly what to do; she unbolted the back door to the kitchen and stepped into the garden. Chester was not laying in his usual bed. He had cowered under the kitchen table. Rachel, in bare feet, slowly started to walk toward a figure, a shadow, it seemed to beckon her. There was a light sound of twigs on the grass, breaking under her soft footsteps. Rachel stopped at the bottom of the archaeological site. Her eyes fixed on the shadow, now a mere ten feet away from Rachel. It beckoned her once more, inviting her forward. She stepped onto the tarpaulin covering, her weight forced one side to collapse. Rachel fell head-first into the grave.

CHAPTER 17 – THE FOLLOWING DAY

Rachel's fall into the grave woke her, with a fright. She screamed, where was she? How did she get there? She fumbled around her new whereabouts. In the dark she came across a skeleton hand; she screamed and screamed, constantly. Chester heard this and barked perpetually. Annie threw on her dressing gown and rushed downstairs. Oh my god, something else has happened she thought. Mr & Mrs Hooper woke and turned their bedside light on. Rachel's sister Rebecca slept through the whole ordeal. Annie grabbed a torch and rushed out into the garden. She followed the screams and sobbing of a distressed young girl. She reached the excavation site. Rachel had fallen into the grave.

'How the hell,' screeched Annie, 'Rachel give me your hand.' Annie pulled Rachel out of the grave; the girl was shaking and trembling. Annie embraced Rachel, 'How ever did you get down there?' asked Annie.

'I'm not sure,' whispered Rachel, still trying to recover from the shock.

Mrs and Mr Hooper arrived simultaneously. 'Rachel, my baby,' cried Mrs Hooper. She took over embracing Rachel from Annie. She gave her the biggest hug. Annie had to explain to Mr & Mrs Hooper that archaeologists had found human remains, they were going to remove them, to laboratory test on Monday.

'Not soon enough,' blurted Mrs Hooper.

'How did your daughter get to the garden?' questioned Annie. She checked her watch, it was 3 am.

Nightmares at Ye Olde Elm Tree

Mrs Hooper looked at Rachel, gave her a squeeze, and asked, 'Were you sleep walking darling?' Rachel shook her head. She did not know for sure, what had just happened.

'I thought I heard my name called, it was as if someone was calling me, to come closer,' Rachel murmured.

Mrs. Hooper looked at Annie and admitted that Rachel used to sleep walk when she was a little girl, but she hasn't for several years, until possibly now. Mr and Mrs Hooper took Rachel back to her bedroom, making sure she was safely back in her bed.

Next morning, Annie was preparing breakfasts for her guests. Mary arrived via the back door, waving a Sunday newspaper. At the foot of the front page of this newspaper, the report read 'MORE MYSTERY LINKED TO YE OLDE ELM TREE.' The report had photographs of all four missing men, the three travelling salesmen, who had rooms reserved at Ye Olde Elm Tree, and the local photographer, looking for a story at the public house and inn. The report was critical of the local constabulary, and covered the unsuccessful excavations of several locations in the pub grounds. It mentioned how the local police had arrested the landlady Annie Baines but failed to charge her. At the foot of the report Annie noticed who the reporter was. It was Nick Fitzsimons.

Annie put a call in to Detective Inspector Judd. She explained in detail how the youngest Hooper daughter had fallen into the grave.

'The tarpaulin is not sufficient cover,' declared Annie, 'What if she sleepwalks again tonight?' construed Annie. DI Judd promised Annie to take supplementary action, with the grave. Annie went on to explain how the Devons' parents called into Ye Olde Elm Tree in the lunch hour. The Inspector admitted to Annie that she wanted to call on them, to see how they were getting on; she promised to visit them that day. As the detective put the phone down on Annie, she picked up a copy of the Sunday newspaper, with the Nick Fitzsimons report. Detective Chief Superintendent Thackeray is going to be upset when he reads this, she thought.

The Woodhall family were first down for breakfast. Fifteen minutes later the Hooper family arrived. Mr Hooper chose a table in the bar quite a distance from the Woodhall's table. Mr Woodhall thought that was a little odd, especially as they all had dinner together the night before.

'Sleep well?' called out Mr Woodhall. There was a pause.

'Not really,' replied Mr Hooper. He explained how Rachel had supposedly slept walked then fell into the grave in the garden. 'Thank goodness she was not hurt,' blurted Mr Hooper. There was silence all around the bar. A discussion followed on how dangerous it was.

Mr Hooper added, 'I hope the landlady has liability insurance.' Mary had overheard the conversation; walked into the kitchen, and informed Annie.

Edgar was down later for breakfast. He was keen for the two families to finish their breakfasts first. Edgar had heard the commotion in the night and had listened to the discussions of the Hooper family and Annie from down the corridor. He sat down with Annie as she poured her heart out once more.

'Annie this is just another hurdle to overcome,' he said delicately, 'Think again about living with me, in New Zealand.'

Annie looked compassionately at Edgar and said 'I would struggle with moving that far away from my sister Nancy, Edgar. We have grown so much closer since Bert tragically died. The Lake District to Dorset is bad enough.'

'Bring her with you,' he implied. 'The more the merrier, it can be very lonely, living on your own.'

The Hooper family climbed down two flights of stairs with their bags and cases; they had chosen to check out. Annie was shocked and disappointed, but this time she could understand why. Annie offered the family a refund for the night they would not be staying. Mr Hooper thanked her, but declined her offer. A possible lawsuit was more on his mind.

DI Judd arrived at the parents' home of Garrett and Gresham Devons. They welcomed the officer into their home and offered her a cup of tea, with biscuits. They were still dismayed by the loss of their two sons and now a nephew. The inspector tactfully questioned the couple on how they were feeling, and coping. Well into the discussion, the inspector mentioned their visit to Ye Olde Elm Tree. Mr Devons explained how Gresham blamed the landlady for Garrett's accident, and how he wanted to get even with her. He explained how they had asked him not to do anything stupid.

'We wanted to see her for ourselves,' said Mr Devons, 'See what kind of woman she was.'

'Who were you with, a young male?' asked DI Judd.

'Oh, that was another nephew of ours, another Devons boy, Richard,' came the answer.

Mary stripped the bedclothes in the Hooper's bedrooms. Annie had promised Edgar a bed for the night, rather than the couch.

Dr Bell and Dr Donnelly arrived at Ye Olde Elm Tree. This is most unheard of to work on a Sunday afternoon, thought Dr Bell. Dr Donnelly was more accustomed to working weekends; some of his archaeological work would go on for weeks, even months. He once had an assignment in Turkey that lasted three years. Ye Olde Elm Tree was having a busy Sunday lunchtime with tourists. Detective Sergeant Roach was the next to arrive and had to park on the road. This old pub is becoming my second home, he thought. Annie watched the sergeant arrive from the pub window. She looked onto the cars parked in the corner of the car park, where she had seen the Mercedes sink into the ground. She prayed there would never be a repeat of that experience.

Contractor George arrived in his truck, also having to park on the road. George had brought a strong piece of plywood to cover the excavation. George was eaten up with curiosity on what had happened with the young girl. He subsequently pumped questions at the sergeant. DS Roach remained evasive with his responses.

The sergeant went to check on the two doctors at the graveside. 'How is it going?' he asked.

'Looks like we will be able to take the skull and one arm back to the lab today. The arm had separated from the main body at the shoulder joint.' replied Dr Donnelly. 'The torso is suffused in muddy soil, so the rest of the body is going to take us longer to exhume.'

The sergeant was curious to how the process works of identifying the age of human remains.

"When you go back to the laboratory, what happens then?" asked DS Roach.

'We use Radiocarbon-dating. By measuring certain radioactive isotopes, through cosmic rays in the atmosphere, nitrogen molecules oxidise to become carbon dioxide.' answered Dr Donnelly. DS Roach looked dumbfound, he did not fully comprehend what Dr Donnelly had just explained.

Dr Bell sensed that and added, 'Humans, when they are alive, consume sources of carbon. When we die, we stop consuming carbon, so we are no longer replenishing, therefore when we are dead it all begins to decay.' The sergeant smiled at Dr Bell and thanked them both for their explanations. What have I just learnt today he asked himself?

The two doctors enclosed the skull and the arm into a carefully prepared ossuary chest. Together with the help of the sergeant, they made sure the plywood covering was securely placed and staked over the grave. Nobody could fall through it this time, they believed.

In the two bedrooms in the roof of Ye Olde Elm Tree, one had a double bed, the other had two single beds. Edgar was back in his single bed for the night. It just so happened, that was the same room Rachel Hooper had shared with her sister. It was also the room where Toby Devons was pushed out of his bedroom window. It was also the room where young Jack Delany heard voices and saw some haunting looking shadows from his bedroom window. Sleeping there did not faze Edgar, he did not believe in the paranormal. It did take him quite a while to fall off to sleep. The rain was lashing down on his bedroom window. At some point during the night he thought he heard voices. He could not make out what the voices were chanting. He strolled over to the window, put on his spectacles, tried staring out of the window but the rain was running down the window in streams, visibility was awful. He stared into the garden toward the grave, beyond that he thought he saw five, possibly six figures stood motionless; what appeared to be several men, a woman, and a child. He deduced that his mind had started to play tricks on him. Edgar went back to bed and tried to go back to sleep. He eventually nodded off, but the voices continued. It was just getting light, the next morning, when Edgar woke with a start. He had a nightmare; he had dreamt of a shadow figure of a man, was stood at the foot of his bed!

CHAPTER 18 – THE ONSLAUGHT

Annie was preparing breakfast for the Woodhall family. This is going to be a normal Monday morning she hoped. After breakfast, cellar work, cleaning the pipes, tap and vent the barrels for the week ahead. She should also receive her emergency beer order that morning. The Woodhall family had breakfast and proceeded to check out.

'Such a shame, that awful incident with the young Hooper girl,' Mr Woodhall implied. Annie smiled and agreed with him, compassionately.

Edgar was later down for breakfast, having had quite a restless night. He asked Annie if he could change rooms, the rain lashing down kept him awake most of the night. Annie was puzzled by his request, but agreed he could go into one of the Woodhall's rooms at the front of the pub. When asked, Edgar did not fancy much breakfast, he just asked for toast, which bemused Annie further. Afterwards Edgar walked the long route to the next village for a newspaper. His mind was racing over the night before. Edgar was only stopping until Friday that week, he had a return flight to New Zealand that weekend. Annie would surely miss Edgar. She enjoyed having him around.

Annie checked the pub diary; all four rooms were let for the following weekend. On the first floor was a Spanish family, the Mendez family. On the top floor was a Mr & Mrs Rocastle and a Mr & Mrs Smith. The latter made Annie smile. When her and Bert first met and they stayed away in a bed and breakfast, on two occasions they gave false names of Mr & Mrs Smith. She wondered if the couple staying this coming weekend were married!

Over a cup of coffee, Mary explained to Annie how there was possibly a new man in her life.

'How interesting, what's he like?' asked Annie.

'His name is Bryan, he's an odd job man at the Llewellyn Country Estate,' replied Mary. 'He hasn't worked there long, three months, he's quite handsome, quite distinguished with flowing grey hair. He is a year younger, but yesterday he hinted we should go out for dinner.'

Annie clutched Mary's hand. 'You should go Mary; how many years has it been since Royston left you?' asked Annie.

'Twenty years,' replied Mary, 'Not that I'm counting.' Mary decided to spring clean the Inglenook fireplace while Annie descended on the cellar.

Reporter Nick Fitzsimons had studied Ye Olde Elm Tree in some detail. He would like to investigate the grave site in the garden, having received word that there was an archaeological excavation taking place. The pub was face on to the road; as you look at the pub the car park is to the right-hand side. The car park has a six-foot stone wall surrounding it. Thanks to Bob Truman's handy work, there is no access to the back garden from the car park, just a lockable gate. On the left-hand side of the pub is a public footpath. Along the footpath the pub garden was protected by a six-foot wooden fence. Nick walked the path to see farmland beyond the garden, a four-foot barb wire fence separating the farmland from the footpath, and the garden.

Nick thought if he had some strong wire cutters, he could gain access to Ye Olde Elm Tree's garden.

Detective Chief Superintendent Thackeray took a call from his director. A television outside broadcast unit were looking to stage an interview with a senior police officer, following the daily tabloid's report on the four missing men, linked to Ye Olde Elm Tree.

'I think you should handle this one yourself Raj,' said the Director. Raj Thackeray put the telephone down, run his fingers through his hair, and reached for the newspaper, to read the report for a second time.

Monday lunchtime trading, Mollie was managing the bar, having to remember the trap door to the cellar was open, where Annie was finishing off her pipe cleaning. Richard Devons entered Ye Olde Elm Tree. He walked straight up to the bar and asked Mollie if she was the landlady.

'No, I'm not,' said Mollie, 'You must be looking for Annie, I will give her a shout.' As Mollie said that Annie came up from the cellar and closed the trap door behind her.

'This gentleman has asked to see you Annie,' said Mollie, pointing at Richard Devons.

'Good day,' he announced, 'My name is Richard Devons and I would like to see where my cousins, Gresham, Garrett and Toby all died.' Annie looked horrified.

'I cannot help you sir,' replied Annie; thoughts of Toby Devons laying the wreaths, flashed through her mind. 'The pub garden; has been declared as an archaeological, historic site, any enquiry is now a matter for the police, perhaps you had better try the local police station; your request is their responsibility. Annie turned to walk out and whispered to Mollie,

'Don't serve him.'

Richard Devons watched Annie leave the bar and decided to order a pint of ale. Mollie explained that she was not allowed to serve him.

'That is preposterous,' he bellowed and stormed out of the pub. Many customers looked on in astonishment.

That morning and lunchtime, Charles Braithwaite visited five public houses. Four of them were reporting a reduction in sales revenue, monthly and quarterly. The fifth public house happened to be one of Charles' favourites, that was merely in a nearby location. Two of the four had experienced rent increases from Charles' company, so unfortunately for Charles, this had dominated the conversations. There was a new mega-store opened up in the local area, selling beers at ridiculously low prices, which was the main gripe of the third public house. The fourth pub announced they were haemorrhaging money, in a spiral debt situation. They needed to sell the lease as quickly as possible. Charles was not surprised, he did not have a great consideration on how it was operating, although saddened by the news. It would mean extra work for Charles, to try and find new tenants.

Charles returned to the office afterwards, to inform his directors. Someone had left a tabloid on his desk. It covered the article on the four missing men. Charles knew all about the three men in the car, although he had formed his own opinion that Annie must have been hallucinating. Did she have mental health issues? Perhaps she was drunk, Charles thought. Charles had not heard of the fourth missing man, the photographer, this may have changed his plans for tomorrow, perhaps he should return to Ye Olde Elm Tree.

Detective Inspector Judd had a prearranged telephone call with a barrister, Donald Rutherford SC, senior counsel, for 3 pm. This is going to be interesting, thought the Inspector, he is not a lawyer or a solicitor, he is a senior counsel that has been appointed to investigate, the three missing salesmen.

'Good afternoon Detective Inspector Judd, Donald Rutherford here, I have been appointed to the case of Foreman, Aylott and Hardwick by solicitors Copthorne and Whatley.'

'Good afternoon Mr Rutherford,' replied the Inspector. 'How can I help you?'

The barrister asked the inspector for her brief on the evening that the three gentlemen allegedly went missing. The inspector briefed the barrister on their conversation with licensee Annie Baines.

'She took near on two weeks to inform the police, that is remarkably controvertible, do you not agree Inspector?' questioned the Barrister. DI Judd agreed totally; she went on to explain the reasons Annie Baines was afraid to notify the authorities.

'So, what happens next?' asked Donald Rutherford SC, his response was quite pressing.

The detective went into detail to explain how the multiple digs at the site, were inconclusive.

'Do you consider this landlady character, Mrs Baines, to be insane, to concoct such a story?' probed the Barrister. DI

Judd carefully dodged that question, by apologising in not being qualified to make that form of judgement.

'What about this photographer fellow, that the press claim is also missing, and linked to that very same public house?' asked Donald Rutherford SC.

The Inspector explained how the excavation was more of a procedure, following the earlier encounter. She then went on to disclose the discovery of the skeleton grave.

'Good Lord,' exclaimed the Donald Rutherford SC. 'A skeleton, archaeological dig, you police folk certainly know how to dig up a pile of worms, so to speak.' He laughed down the telephone. DI Judd was far from amused.

Nick Fitzsimons visited his local DIY store. He hired a high-quality bolt cutter, with an 80mm cutting diameter. These will do the job, Nick thought. He set his alarm that night for 1 am. He drove over to Ye Olde Elm Tree and parked up in the layby, close by. He put on a sturdy pair of walking boots. There had been so much rain of late, he anticipated Annie's garden might be muddy in places. He walked up the footpath and proceeded to cut through the farm fence, with ease. He checked for any sounds or movement coming from the pub, there was an eerie silence. He cut through the second fence and entered the garden. He realised the ground was slushy. He shone his torch around the garden, the sound of an owl spooked him momentarily. His torch shone on the boarded-up grave. He was disappointed, a plywood covered grave would not make a great photograph for a story, after he had gone to so much trouble. His torch then caught site of a moving figure. Where did it go? Nick asked himself. He saw another moving figure, it also seemed to disappear into the night.

Nightmares at Ye Olde Elm Tree

At that moment, he heard a frightening sound of birds squawking. An unkindness of ravens came swooping down toward him. They brushed his shoulder. A murder of crows followed, swooping down toward him, they brushed his jacket on the arm, another brushed his hair. Nick started to run back to the footpath, swinging his wire cutters in the air to protect himself from the birds attacking him. It was heavy going and hard work to run on the wet and slippery grass. The ground seemed muddier than before. The birds continued to attack him until, he finally reached the footpath. There was no longer any sign of attacking birds. He drew his breath for a moment, he was aghast. Nick could hear a dog barking from the direction of the pub, it was Chester. Nick ran back to his car, started the engine and in muddy boots, drove erratically home

CHAPTER 19 – TRAUMATISED

Reporter Nick Fitzsimons arrived home in quite a state. He took his muddy boots off at the front door; took his jacket off and noticed a sizeable rip in his jeans, he was wearing grey chinos. Nick remembered he caught his trousers on the garden fence scrabbling to get out of the reach of those aggressive birds. Those birds! reflected Nick, and those figures that disappeared, that was mad, beyond belief! Nick decided to clamber back into bed, his jeans were destined for the bin.

Next morning Annie ventured downstairs to discover Chester was quite anxious, agitated, pacing the kitchen. Annie let Chester out of the back door, he went running down the bottom of the garden. Annie put on her gardening shoes and followed Chester. He was sat by the fence whimpering. Annie suddenly noticed that someone had cut through her boundary wire fence. She looked across to the footpath, they had cut through the farmer's fence too. She turned and looked at the boarded-up grave, that seemed intact.

'Good heavens Chester, I had better phone the police,' cried Annie.

Annie telephoned Detective Inspector Judd and informed her of the break-in to her garden.

'Was there any interference with the excavation?' asked the Inspector.

'No, that looked untouched,' came the reply. Annie went on to tell the inspector about the visit she had from Richard Devons, another cousin, and what he had asked.

'I'll try and locate Richard Devons,' said the Inspector. 'We'll also try and drop by Ye Olde Elm Tree and take a look at the break-in.' DI Judd put the phone down and called across the office to Detective Sergeant Roach,

'We need to hit the road again Sergeant, make another call on Ye Olde Elm Tree.' DS Roach shook his head. Leaving the office, DI Judd asked one of her detective constables to check out a cousin to the Devons family, named Richard, where he lived and where he might be staying in the local area, in a hotel, or bed and breakfast.

DI Judd and DS Roach arrived at Ye Olde Elm Tree. Annie walked them down to the bottom of the garden to show them the damaged fence.

'There are traces of footprints,' claimed the Inspector.

'They are more defined on Granville's farmland,' pointed out Annie. The sergeant noticed a piece of grey material on the fence.

'Looks like the intruder has left us a clue,' said the Sergeant.

'I will call forensic, Mrs Baines, they can take photographic evidence of the footprints and take the material away for analysis,' confirmed DI Judd.

Before the police officers had left, Dr Bell and Dr Donnelly had arrived at Ye Olde Elm Tree to conclude their exhumation. The five exchanged pleasantries, then Dr Bell informed the officers that the early indication from artefacts analysed in the laboratory so far, suggested a middle-aged woman, buried approximately 130-140 years ago.

'We have a Victorian aged corpse,' claimed Dr Bell.

DI Judd thanked Dr Bell. Before they returned to the police car, the inspector informed the doctors that Detective Chief Superintendent Thackeray would like to expand on the unearthing. They have dug only where the photographer's camera was found, so far. On the discovery of the historic grave, and bearing in mind the location of the camera may not be aligned to the photographer's disappearance, the superintendent would like to start a second dig.

'We will need to put a new permit in place,' proclaimed Dr Bell.

'Can you drop by the station later? We will need to get this organised, without haste,' asked the Inspector.

DI Judd took a call on her mobile from her detective constable back at the station.

'Richard Devons lives in the Midlands, Ma'am. He is staying locally at the Hermitage bed and breakfast. Do you need me to send you the post code Ma'am?' asked DC Brentwood.

'That's ok Liz, I know where the Hermitage is, thank you, Liz,' replied the Inspector. It is a haven for druggies and reprobates, thought the detective.

It was almost time for Annie to open up the pub for the lunchtime trading when Charles Braithwaite arrived at Ye Olde Elm Tree. Charles was wearing his navy blue, pin-stripe suit, red tie, red top pocket handkerchief and red framed glasses.

'Good morning Annie,' bellowed Charles as if he was Annie's best friend.

'Good morning Charles,' said Annie. 'I did not expect to see you so soon.'

Charles had heard about the missing photographer, and he wondered how an archaeological excavation had developed. Annie invited Charles into the back garden.

'You can meet the two doctors carrying out the excavation, if you like?' she suggested. Charles' eyes lit up, how wonderful he thought.

Annie introduced Charles to the two doctors. They explained to Charles, their findings so far, middle-aged female, Victorian corpse. Charles was speechless.

'We are planning to start a second excavation in the same localised area,' explained Dr Donnelly.

'But surely you will have to get my company's permission to do that?' barked Charles. 'My company owns the public house and the grounds.'

'We have a permit to start the excavation,' said Dr Donnelly, tongue in cheek.

'Permit?' questioned Charles.

'Yes, the permit for this current excavation would have been sent onto the Chief of Police, Land Registry and the current land-owner's CEO.

Charles retreated slightly. He turned to Annie and enquired 'You did not tell me all this was going on Annie,' as if to delegate responsibility.

'Sorry Charles, but I have a busy pub to run.' She patted Chester on the head and summoned him back in the direction of the pub.

DI Judd and DS Roach arrived at Nick Fitzsimons' home. Outside the front door was a pair of muddy walking boots. 'Sergeant, bag them up before we knock the door for entry,' instructed the Inspector.

'But Guv, we should not,' responded the Sergeant.

DI Judd interrupted, 'Sergeant, our credibility is at stake here, we need to find some dependable evidence to these disappearances, and now this break-in, at Ye Olde Elm Tree.'

Having bagged up the boots and put them in the boot of his police car, DS Roach knocked the door of Nick Fitzsimons' home. It took a while for him to come to the door; when he finally answered, he looked dreadful, as if someone who had not slept all night.

'May we come in Mr Fitzsimons?' enquired DI Judd, 'We would like to update you on where we are with the missing Gordon McLarty investigation.' He reluctantly asked the two officers into his home.

DI Judd explained how the dig for Mr McLarty had evolved into an archaeological unearthing. She also explained that the police department have authorised further excavations. Nick was torn, bemused, the police seemed to be doing what they could, but his friend Gordon was still mysteriously missing, then he had encountered that terrible tribulation with the birds in the pub garden. It was then that DI Judd pounced on the reporter,

'Mr Fitzsimons, have you returned to Ye Olde Elm Tree at all since your friend's disappearance?' she asked. 'Did you visit Ye Olde Elm Tree in the early hours of last night?'

Nick Fitzsimons' face froze. He looked agitated. The reporter admitted to his daytime visit to the old inn but stayed inexplicit to any night-time visit. That said it all to the inspector, his reactions gave him away. The officers bid Nick Fitzsimons good day and left.

Mary finished her shift at Ye Olde Elm Tree and announced to Annie that the new man in her life, Bryan, was meeting her there. Mary was keen to introduce Bryan to Annie. He seemed very attentive and caring toward Mary. The sucker punch came at the close of their conversation,

'If there are any odd jobs that you need attending to, Bryan is your man,' suggested Mary. That could be awkward with Bob Truman's loyalty to her, thought Annie.

DI Judd and DS Roach visited local farmer Granville Warren. His farmland backed onto Ye Olde Elm Tree garden. The officers explained about the break-in through his perimeter fence. They informed the farmer that they may have a suspect. Granville thanked them and promised he would have a look at the damaged fence, that day. He also thought he would call in on Annie. Being a regular at Ye Olde Elm Tree, Granville had a lot of admiration for Annie.

DI Judd and DS Roach then drove to the Hermitage bed and breakfast. The décor left a lot to be desired, thought the inspector, to the extent that she would not like to sleep there! The receptionist was extremely helpful; DI Judd recognised the receptionist from a previous conviction. He explained to the officers that Richard Devons had gone to the local railway station to pick up his wife; indicating he should return to the bed and breakfast quite soon. The officers decided to go in search of some fast food, and return to the Hermitage later; it had been a busy day so far.

Dr Bell and Dr Donnelly were finishing off at the graveside. All the remaining artefacts had been carefully stored in three ossuary chests. They thanked Annie for the much-appreciated teas and coffees. Dr Bell telephoned DS Roach to inform him that their unearthing had concluded. The sergeant, in turn, telephoned police contractor George.

'We are on tomorrow George, for a second dig at Ye Olde Elm Tree. Bring the mini-digger, I will try and get there for 9 am,' said the Sergeant. George was ecstatic, another dig for a possible body, he helped himself to a beer out of the fridge.

DI Judd and DS Roach returned to the Hermitage. On entry, the receptionist rang through to Richard Devons' bedroom.

'Hello sir, you have some visitors in reception.' He did not say who, he was quick to put the phone down, he was extremely nervous. Richard Devons appeared with his wife Catheryn; he had a horrified look on his face, when he saw two police officers.

'Can we have a quick chat?' asked DI Judd, 'Perhaps outside, in the garden?' The four of them settled in the Hermitage garden. DI Judd acknowledged Richard Devons' visit to Ye Olde Elm Tree, which surprised Richard; his reaction was that the landlady had squealed on him, what a bitch he thought. The Inspector explained that there were some archaeological digs taking place at Ye Olde Elm Tree over the next few days. It might be in everyone's interest not to visit the public house whilst this work was ongoing.

With that said, Catheryn stood up and bawled, 'We don't have to listen to this crap Rich, we can go where we want, whenever we want.' Richard and Catheryn departed from the officers and returned to their residence.

'I think she is going to be trouble Sergeant,' murmured the Inspector.

The card school at Ye Olde Elm Tree met once more on the Tuesday evening, including Edgar; this would be his last appearance, before heading back to New Zealand. Jules, Badger and Norm had decided to teach Edgar how to play cribbage. By the end of the evening Edgar had mastered the game quite well. He was delighted to be on the winning side with his partner Julian Jameson.

Reporter Nick Fitzsimons had another restless night. The bird attacks were haunting him. His alarm went off at 7.30 am but he felt dreadful. He telephoned a local newspaper to tell them he might not make it into the office that day. There was a banging on his front door. Nick scrambled to his bedroom window and looked down; it was DI Judd and DS Roach.

'What do they want?' he cursed. Nick quickly made himself presentable and answered the door.

'Good morning Mr Fitzsimons,' said the Inspector, 'We have a warrant to search your premises, may we come in?' The officers stepped into the hall. The reporter was dumbfounded.

'Search warrant, what's this all about?' asked Nick Fitzsimons.

'We believe you broke into the grounds of Ye Olde Elm Tree on....' The inspector read the details of the permit to the reporter. 'Sergeant, you look upstairs, I will look downstairs,' suggested the Inspector. They both went about their search, when Nick Fitzsimons suddenly remembered his muddy boots were at the front door. He sneaked to the door, opened it, to discover they were no longer there. That was uncanny, he had not moved them. His mind was racing, again.

DI Judd lifted the lid of a bin in the kitchen. Scrolled up was a pair of grey chinos. The inspector put on a pair of latex gloves, removed the trousers from the bin and bagged them for her forensic team. They were ripped. The Inspector called up the stairs,

'It's ok Sergeant, you can come down now, we have found what we are looking for.' Nick Fitzsimons looked stunned.

'What do you want with my trousers?' he asked.

'Would you like to tell me where exactly you ripped your trousers Mr Fitzsimons?' enquired DI Judd. It fell silent. DS Roach returned to the ground floor; DI Judd showed the sergeant the bagged up, ripped grey trousers. The sergeant nodded with his approval. The Inspector turned and announced to the reporter,

'Mr Fitzsimons, we are arresting you, in accordance with the Criminal Damage Act of 1971, where you, without lawful excuse, recklessly caused damage to two properties, with an intent to cause aggravated trespass, to an archaeological historic site. You **do** not have to say anything, but it may harm your defence, if you **do** not mention when questioned, something which you later rely on **in** court. Anything you do say, may be given in evidence.' The sergeant cuffed Nick Fitzsimons. As they left the house,

Nick asked if they had taken a pair of walking boots, that were by his front door.

'Yes, we have those down at the station,' replied the Sergeant, 'They are helping us with our enquiries.'

CHAPTER 20 – STRIKING FOR GOLD

That evening, Ye Olde Elm Tree darts team were away to the top of the league, Burton Arms. Some of the team were a little apprehensive, the opposition had two County players in their team. It was 10.45 pm, Annie was just looking at the clock, to call last orders, when the darts team came back into Ye Olde Elm Tree. Annie only had to look at their faces, they have lost, she thought. Team captain Charlie (Chas) Hind was the first to the bar.

'How did it go?' asked Annie.

'Lost seven – nil,' said Chas 'it was a bit of a beating.'

'A whitewash I think you call it?' joked Annie. Chas rallied the team, calling for extra practices between then, and next week when Ye Olde Elm Tree play the Burton Arms again, at home.

Detective Sergeant Roach arrived the next morning at Ye Olde Elm Tree just before 9 am. Contractor George arrived soon after, with his mini digger on the back of his truck.

'Morning George,' said the Sergeant. 'First thing we need to do, is take out one of those new fence panels, so we can manoeuvre the mini digger into the back garden.' George could see the task ahead and acknowledged the policeman.

Detective Inspector Judd received a telephone message via the City of Glasgow Police Department, from initially Gordon McLarty's ex-wife Moira. She was still missing the child maintenance money from her ex-husband, Gordon. This frustrated the inspector.

'So, we are a child maintenance complaints department now, are we?' she scorned to herself.

To add to the Detective's frustrating morning, she met Detective Chief Superintendent Thackeray at the office water cooler.

'How did it go sir, with the television interview?' she asked. He looked at the inspector with contempt.

'Rita, I never want to be put through that agony again,' came his reply. 'What could I tell them? Sweet FA! We must make some ground on these missing people soon, or I will have to take you off the case Rita.' The superintendent returned to his office.

Edgar had breakfast with Annie. She told him about the second excavation.

'You really don't need this, Annie,' said Edgar. 'Did you talk to Nancy about New Zealand?' he asked.

'No, sorry Edgar, it's been so hectic, just of late, I will call her today,' promised Annie. They both got tucked into their smoked salmon, scrambled eggs and roasted asparagus.

Charles Braithwaite read his email; another of the public houses that he manages tendered a resignation on their tenancy contract. He reflected on the pub's performance over the last twelve months. They once had a turnover of four part-time chefs, and multiple kitchen staff. The landlady had become the cook in the kitchen, serving what she described as; home cooked food. The standard had dropped, so had the custom. Charles reflected on how he advised them to keep on a quality chef; rising costs may have clouded their judgement. That is sad, he thought, and more work for him. Charles sent an email to his board of directors about the Victorian corpse, at Ye Olde Elm Tree, which was probably in the tabloids by now, he thought. Also, the police announcing further excavations at Ye Olde Elm Tree. His email was slightly biased. He emphasised the increased tourist trade that would surely deliver.

Contractor George had started the dig. Left and right of the Victorian relic's grave. DS Roach joined him.

'No sign of the photographer's body yet Sergeant,' called George over the noise of his machine. 'I have dug down four feet either side of the grave.' The police officer examined the dig.

'Keep going George" instructed DS Roach.

Nick Fitzsimons was interviewed by Detective Inspector Rita Judd and Detective Constable Liz Brentwood. DI Judd recorded the time and stated the reason for the interview. She asked for his compendium on what happened on the night in question.

'I only wanted to take a few photographs of the archaeological grave,' admitted Nick Fitzsimons. 'It was not something I would normally do,' he continued. 'I would normally ask Gordon McLarty to acquire photographs for my newspaper reports. I set the alarm and drove over to Ye Olde Elm Tree in the middle of the night. I knew I would have to cut through the farm fence, and garden fence, to gain access to the pub garden. I walked over to the archaeological site and was disappointed, it was battened down with a plywood cover, nothing to photograph really. Then I heard a squawking. Hundreds of birds started to attack me.' Nick started to raise his voice.

'Hundreds of birds?' enquired the Inspector.

'Sorry,' Nick Fitzsimons gathered his thoughts. 'There must have been a flock of twenty, thirty birds that attacked me, brushed my shoulder. Then a different flock of birds attacked me, hit my arm, hit my hair, I had to run for it, it was awful.' Nick became emotional.

'What kind of birds were they?' asked the Detective.

'Ghastly big black birds, I'm not sure, rooks, jackdaws, crows, ravens, it was horrible, it was horrible.' Nick Fitzsimons became hysterical. DI Judd tried to calm him down.

'Can I get you a glass of water?' she asked. He acknowledged the Inspector.

'Yes please,' he answered, and started to calm down. 'But there is more!' exclaimed Nick. 'I was sure I saw two black figures, like shadows, appear and then disappear. The old inn is haunted if you ask me, there is no other explanation,' concluded Nick Fitzsimons. DI Judd made a note of the time and terminated the recording.

'We'll fetch a glass of water for you Mr Fitzsimons,' the Inspector reassured him. Leaving the room, DC Brentwood said to her Inspector,

'That was all a bit weird, don't you think Ma'am? Haunted! Flocks of birds! Shadows!'

'Well at least we have a confession,' replied DI Judd.

It was lunchtime trading at Ye Olde Elm Tree. Annie had to make a dash to the local superstore. She was still running out of supplies, being busier than normal. Vodka, gin, whiskey, crisps, amongst other things. Mollie and Jimmy covered the bar while Annie was shopping. Unexpectantly, Richard Devons and his wife Catheryn entered Ye Olde Elm Tree. Jimmy served them as he was not aware that they were barred by Annie. They sat down at a table in the bar; Mollie spotted them, she became anxious. She explained the situation to Jimmy and put in a call to Annie's mobile. That was the last thing Annie wanted to hear. She in turn telephoned DI Judd.

Detective Inspector Judd received a telephone call from Donald Rutherford SC, enquiring how the excavation was proceeding. The Inspector briefed the barrister on the age of the artefact and how a further excavation had started that day.

'Splendid, do try and find those missing men with your endeavours Inspector,' said Donald Rutherford SC, with a hearty laugh. DI Judd hung up the phone. There was something irritating about that barrister, she thought, she hoped she would never have to meet him in court.

Richard and Catheryn Devons ventured into the pub car park with their drink; they both lit up cigarettes. They walked over to where the fence panel had been taken out and glared into the pub's back garden where George was manipulating his next dig. Annie arrived back at Ye Olde Elm Tree in her Morris Minor. She took her shopping out of the boot and noticed Richard Devons with a female staring at the back garden. They both turned around and looked at Annie.

'I am really sorry,' said Annie, 'No more drinks I'm afraid, you are barred, so I would like you to please drink up and leave.' Annie started to walk towards the front door of the pub. She heard a glass smash on the ground.

'Bitch,' shouted Catheryn. Annie kept on walking; she never looked back.

Charles Braithwaite was tidying up his desk in the office, time to go home he thought. He received an alert of a new email, from his director Douglas Winterbottom. The Board had held a conference call and Douglas was elected to pay a personal visit to Ye Olde Elm Tree, somewhat of a publicity stunt for the pub company. Charles was asked to accompany Douglas. Charles thought, how could he decline? He replied and asked Douglas Winterbottom to choose a suitable date and time.

Detective Sergeant Roach returned to the Ye Olde Elm Tree. Richard Devons was just finishing his drink. DI Judd had just telephoned the sergeant; she implied that the Devons couple might be at Ye Olde Elm Tree. He should try and ask them to leave, was her advice. DS Roach spotted them both in the corner of the car park, and approached them.

'Good day, Richard, good day, Catheryn,' said the Sergeant. There was no response back, just glares.

'We only wanted to see the locations where Gresham, Garrett and Toby were found dead,' piped-up Richard.

'I have no idea where that is,' replied the Sergeant, tongue in cheek, 'So it really isn't worth staying here, I'm afraid.' He noticed the broken glass on the floor, with a stain of red wine on the gravel floor. 'That's a shame Catheryn, did you drop your drink?' the Sergeant asked. There was no reply, just a scornful look.

'What's he digging for?' asked Richard, pointing at George. The officer sought a reply.

'It has become an archaeological site. Some old artefacts have been found, nothing more,' answered DS Roach. 'Now if I could ask you both to kindly move on?' Richard finished his drink and presented his empty glass to the sergeant. The officer took it and watched the pair return to their vehicle. As they drove off, Catheryn wound her window down and shouted,

'Bastard coppers!' Sadly, it was the type of abuse, that the DS had heard before.

DS Roach joined George, who was progressing well with his excavation. The officer watched him for ten minutes, or more. Suddenly George stopped his engine, peered out of his window and shouted,

'We've struck gold Sergeant. I've hit a second coffin.'

CHAPTER 21 – BULLSEYE

The news of finding a second coffin soon spread around the local police station. Detective Chief Superintendent Thackeray asked Detective Inspector Judd to notify Dr Bell, to see if she and Dr Donnelly could return to Ye Olde Elm Tree the following day. Dr Bell received the news with great excitement; she in turn telephoned Dr Donnelly.

'David, do you have any archaeologist colleagues that can help with this latest unearthing?' she asked.

'I can make a few phone calls Cynthia,' came his reply. 'I might be able to persuade Doctor Adrian Bunce, he is a good friend of mine and I believe he is home, writing a book for the Home University Library.'

'Very good,' said Dr Bell, 'All hands to the pump, so to speak, would be most useful.'

DCS Thackeray called DI Judd into his office.

'Have a seat Rita,' said the Superintendent 'What do you think, if we continued to dig at Ye Olde Elm Tree?' The Inspector thought about how to answer her superior officer.

'Do you think we might find more artefacts sir?' she asked.

'I have no idea Rita, but continued activity at this location may help to divert the media's attention, possibly buy us more time,' came his reply. 'We should take the initiative. We must also respect Dr Bell's efforts with the new grave found. Work in a different location from their current exhumation.'

'What about the landlady and the pub company, they may object,' stated DI Judd.

'We shall put a permit in place for multiple random excavations, they will not be in a position to contest that,' he replied.

Richard and Catheryn Devons checked out of the Hermitage bed and breakfast. The receptionist enquired if they were going home. The couple were quite evasive, being careful not to divulge their plans.

Annie telephoned her sister Nancy. She explained all about the archaeological dig, the female skeleton found, now a second excavation and a second coffin. She had welcomed Bert's brother Edgar staying with her, at Ye Olde Elm Tree; he had been so supportive with everything going on.

'He has suggested I walk away from this old pub, walk away from all of its troubles. He has suggested I sell up and travel to New Zealand and live in the west wing of his home, no strings attached,' she informed Nancy. The phone went silent. 'When I told Edgar, I could not leave you Nancy, his answer was for you to come with me, to New Zealand, start a new life,' announced Annie. 'You don't have to answer me now Nancy, it's just that Edgar is due to fly home this Friday,' said Annie.

'Is selling the pub viable with everything that is going on?' asked Nancy.

'I have no idea,' replied Annie, 'probably not.'

DI Judd telephoned neighbouring farmer Granville and landlady Annie Baines asking if they wanted to press charges for the criminal damage to their properties. She informed them both that reporter Nick Fitzsimons had confessed to the break-in. Much to the Detective's disappointment, both their answers were no to pressing charges, providing he covered the cost of the fences being repaired.

Charles Braithwaite took a telephone call from his director Douglas Winterbottom. Douglas had arranged for a photographer from the Star News to join them at Ye Olde Elm Tree at 2 pm. Great, thought Charles, although that did upend his day somewhat.

Dr Bell and Dr Donnelly arrived at Ye Olde Elm Tree. They carefully removed the plywood covering that George had positioned over the new grave. The mini excavator bucket had broken the coffin lid into two sections. Dr Donnelly very carefully removed the top section of the coffin lid. It exposed a male skeleton upper body and skull. He then carefully removed the second section of the coffin lid.

'It looks very similar in age to the previous artefact,' commented Dr Donnelly.

Without pressing charges, DI Judd announced to Nick Fitzsimons that he was free to go. Both the farmer and the publican would not press charges, providing that Mr Fitzsimons would meet the cost of repairing the fences that he had damaged. He agreed to those repairs.

'Make sure you keep to your word,' scorned the Inspector as Nick Fitzsimons signed the station register, for his release.

Friday morning, it was time for Edgar to head back to the airport to catch his flight back to New Zealand. He was up early, so was Annie to cook him bacon sandwiches for the journey south. Edgar and Annie hugged at the front door. 'My offer will always be there Annie,' said Edgar. She smiled.

'I have mentioned it to Nancy,' came her reply.

'What did she say?' asked Edgar.

'Nancy has always been pragmatic, she reminded me how difficult it might be to sell the lease at Ye Olde Elm Tree,' chuckled Annie. Edgar smiled and walked to his hire car, started the engine, and drove out of the pub car park with a wave of the hand. Annie wondered if she would ever see Edgar again.

The Mendez family arrived at Ye Olde Elm Tree that same morning. The children were quite excited. Lorenzo seven, Liliana five, the family were from northern Spain, San Sebastian. They were all staying on the first floor with Annie. It did not take them long to learn of the unearthing in the back garden. Lorenzo was persistent, he wanted to see the excavation. Annie gave in and took the family into the garden to meet the two doctors. The Mendez family were introduced, the skeleton was very visible. The torso was concealed, buried into the ground.

'I don't like it Mummy,' said little Liliana. Her mother decided to take her daughter back into the pub. Lorenzo was quite the opposite, he was captivated.

Doctor Adrian Bunce arrived at Ye Olde Elm Tree; he introduced himself to Annie. She was not surprised he was an archaeologist; he resembled a mad professor! Annie led Dr Bunce to the garden, where the others were working. Dr Donnelly welcomed his friend with a mud-covered handshake.

Mr and Mrs Rocastle were the next to check-in. They were on the top floor in the double bedroom. Detective Sergeant Roach arrived next, to check if there was any progress. The archaeological team would remove many artefacts that day, but it was agreed to seal the grave and return the next day. DS Roach stood roadside outside the pub and telephoned contractor George.

'We are going to do a few more random digs George,' said the officer, 'We can start either Monday or Tuesday, next week.' DS Roach was about to leave when Richard and Catheryn Devons parked outside Ye Olde Elm Tree. It was to have one last look, before they would head home. The Sergeant noticed their arrival and was adamant, they should not stop at Ye Olde Elm Tree, and to move on. Much to their disgust they drove off, wheels spinning, Catheryn shouting more abuse through her car window.

At 2 pm, Charles Braithwaite, Douglas Winterbottom, and Star News photographer, Eamon Fuller, arrived at Ye Olde Elm Tree. Douglas was in his element. Charles pulled Annie aside and quietly whispered to her not to worry, this was just a publicity stunt for his pub company. Photographs were taken outside and inside the pub, but more importantly, in the garden, with the three doctors and the burial site with the quite visible human remains.

The three doctors and DS Roach made the graveside safe and secure with a second plywood board that contractor George had dropped off, plus a well battened down gazebo, with heavy rain forecast for the night ahead. They all agreed to reconvene the following morning, despite it being a weekend. This disinterment had proven to be a principal unearthing.

Mr and Mrs Smith arrived just before opening time. Annie smiled, remembering her past antics. She showed the young couple to their room in the roof, with the two single beds. Annie smiled once more.

The Friday was without incident, or so Annie thought. Mr Smith announced they were going to check out after breakfast.

'Was there a problem with the room?' asked Annie.

'We had a dreadful night sleeping,' he replied, 'We kept hearing voices from the garden, couldn't see anything with the rain lashing down. We both heard knocking, on our door, on the wall, on the window. Tell me, is this old inn haunted?' asked Mr Smith. Annie was the one to look most ghost-like!

'There have been a few unexplainable circumstances, over the years, but haunted?' Annie said shrugging her shoulders, biting her cheek. The young Smith couple asked for a refund.

Mary arrived whilst breakfast was cooking with a copy of the Star News. Annie and Ye Olde Elm Tree were front page news again. That was quick work, Annie thought.

The Rocastle couple were first down to breakfast, changed, and out for the day sightseeing, quite early. After breakfast, the Mendez children were playing in the car park while Mr and Mrs Mendez packed bags for the day's touring ahead. The heavy rain from the night before had eased, it was an overcast day, with a ten percent chance of rain forecast. Lorenzo wanting to see the grave again, entered the back garden through the missing fence panel, and unzipped the gazebo. Liliana was afraid and ran back into Ye Olde Elm Tree to warn her parents. Mr Mendez, in a state of panic, ran downstairs to find Lorenzo jumping up and down on the plywood grave covering. 'Para Lorenzo,' his Father shouted. In his anxiety, he shouted for the boy to stop, instinctively in Spanish.

The three doctors arrived at Ye Olde Elm Tree soon afterwards. They agreed to work under canvas with the possibility of rain. It was cramped conditions, but exhilarating work.

Annie reflected on the Smiths leaving the accommodation. That room they were in, on the top floor. Edgar asked to move. Toby Devons fell out or was pushed out of the window. Young Jack Delany hearing voices and now the Smith couple, troubled by unexplainable noises. This nightmare is not going to stop, thought Annie. She checked the diary for the following weekend; a Chinese family were booked in, six children, every room filled. My goodness, thought Annie. She decided she would ring the Chen family and enquire on the children's ages. She would give the top room to the eldest children, she deliberated.

The remainder of the weekend was thankfully incident free. Annie gave a sigh of relief. She went about her normal Monday morning chores with the cellar work, choosing to ignore the telephone, which rang relentlessly. Television crews from two separate networks were due to arrive by midday. The three doctors had promised to finish the exhumation that day. Annie decided she was not going to get involved this time, just leave them to it.

On the Tuesday, the third excavation was underway on a different location, to no avail. DS Roach and George decided to down tools at 4 pm. George would leave his mini digger in the garden, to recommence the following day. Annie looked around the garden with Chester before opening time.

'It's starting to look like a bomb site, our poor garden Chester,' Annie said woefully. Tuesday evening saw many regulars, including the card school, although only the three players; they were missing Edgar.

Torrential rain held up the excavation on the Wednesday. The tail end of an American hurricane was hitting the coastline. Trade at Ye Olde Elm Tree was noticeably affected.

Wednesday evening was the return darts match with the Burton Arms. Ye Olde Elm Tree was extremely busy. Even Jimmy was called in to help at the bar. Annie had cooked sausages for the two teams; this was out of character for Annie. The home team was hoping not to receive another thrashing, as they did the previous week. The Burton Arms were three–nil up when Terry Thornley, TT to his friends, stepped up to throw for Ye Olde Elm Tree. Terry was a taxi driver, who took his work very seriously. His wife Karen always dropped him off and collected him on darts nights, so he could have a few beers. The darts team would often mock TT regarding his door to door taxi service. To finish, Terry needed forty-eight. His opponent double eight. His opponent threw first, eight, four, two, leaving him double one to finish. Terry could not believe his luck. Sixteen, double sixteen, he had won. Massive cheers went up for the home team, it was as if they had just won the league.

In the final game, with the Burton Arms winning five–one, the two captains faced each other; Chas Hind for Ye Olde Elm Tree and Ruben Hagen for the opposition. Ruben, who worked on the assembly line of a local electronics factory, was originally from Germany. He was without doubt the most tattooed gent in the pub that night. Ruben won his game, finishing with double top. He removed his darts from the board, held them in the air, with both arms raised, showing off his tattoos in his white vest T-shirt. He welcomed the accreditation from his team-mates.

Ruben decided to walk a lap of honour around the bar with his hands raised. Desmond People and Alice were stood at the bar; they had stayed to watch the darts match that evening. Ruben jeered at Alice.

'Don't you think I am beautiful?' he said in her face. Desmond wanted to punch him. Ruben's eighteen stone frame discouraged him. Ruben returned to the dartboard, threw three darts at the bullseye. One dart hit the bullseye. Suddenly that dart appeared to be thrown back at Ruben. No one was near the dart! It hit Ruben in the face. He crumbled to the ground. He rolled around in agony. The two dart teams watched on in awe.

'My eye, my eye!' Ruben yelled. 'Who the hell threw that dart?' he screeched. Annie watched on in dismay, so did everyone else in the pub; she immediately telephoned for an ambulance.

CHAPTER 22 – MYSTIFIED

The next morning, Annie cooked herself tomatoes on toast for breakfast and sat down with Mary, over a coffee. Annie explained about the build-up and the freak accident to the Burton Arms captain.

'He was an unpleasant character, but did not deserve what happened to him, it was grotesque,' explained Annie, 'What made it worse, the ambulance took fifteen minutes to reach here, the poor guy was rolling on the floor in agony, there was nothing anyone in the pub could do!' Mary consoled Annie.

'There have been some horrible accidents here recently Annie, I don't know how you cope with it all,' answered Mary. Annie told Mary how Edgar would like her to sell up and join him in New Zealand.

'Sell up. Would you Annie?' asked Mary.

'I don't know what to do, for the best,' she replied. Mary suddenly feared for her future at Ye Olde Elm Tree.

Annie telephoned Detective Inspector Judd and informed her of yesterday evening's freak accident.

'Thank you for letting me know Annie,' came the reply, 'I will ask my detective constable to ring the hospital.'

Annie was worried about the forthcoming weekend, so she telephoned the Chen family who were booked to stay at Ye Olde Elm Tree. Mrs Chen came to phone, and Annie asked her the ages of her children. Mrs Chen went into considerable detail.

'My daughter Ju, which means chrysanthemum, is twenty-three. Daughter Liling, meaning white jasmine, twenty-one. Son Fan, meaning mortal, is nineteen. Son Gang, meaning strong, and good, is eighteen. Youngest son Huang, meaning imperial, and majestic, is eight. Youngest daughter Lan, meaning orchid, is seven.' Annie thanked her for such detail, then wondered why the ten-year age gap. She wondered what the Chens were up to for ten years? Annie put the phone down and concluded that the two eldest girls should stay in the top room, with the two single beds.

DI Judd took a call on her mobile from DC Liz Brentwood.

'Good morning Ma'am, it's Liz. I have spoken to the hospital, and the injured dart player Ruben Hagen has a damaged cornea, which they explained to be a transparent window that doubles as a protective covering to the eye. They are considering a protein called Vascular Endothelial Growth Factor (VEGF), which is naturally produced after an eye injury, which can help the cornea to recover. The hospital did say however, that there is a risk with the full recovery of patients sight in that eye.' reported DC Brentwood.

'Thank you, Liz,' replied the Inspector. 'We will need to get statements from everyone that was there yesterday evening. Can you check with the Burton Arms, and Mrs Baines at Ye Olde Elm Tree, and acquire the names and contacts of the two dart teams? Also check with Mrs Baines for any locals in attendance yesterday evening. We will need to get statements from everyone.'

'On the case Ma'am,' came the reply.

Charles Braithwaite signed off another emergency beer order from Ye Olde Elm Tree. He rubbed his hands together in elation. Later he noticed there was no order from the Burton Arms. He telephoned landlord Teddy Valentine, to ask him if he required a beer order.

'Hello Charles. Sorry, it has been chaotic, just of late.' answered Teddy. 'Did you hear what happened to my darts captain last night down at Ye Olde Elm Tree?' Charles went silent, the very mention of Ye Olde Elm Tree seemed to raise the hairs on the back of his neck.

'No Teddy, what happened?' asked Charles worryingly.

'He threw the dart at the bullseye; bloody dart flew back at him. Hit him in the eye! He is in hospital now. I tell you Charles, that old pub is haunted. It has got to be. All the dart team came back here afterwards and swore no one was near the dart board to throw that dart at poor Ruben. Now the police want statements from everyone, including me.'

'That sounds appalling,' replied Charles. 'I will phone the landlady at Ye Olde Elm Tree, see what she has to say for herself. Oh, by the way, beer order?' asked Charles.

'Yes, sorry Charles, I will do it now,' confirmed Teddy.

Thursday, the weather was heavy rain. No dig for poor George, that day. He sat in his little unit, playing Solitaire, Candy Crush Saga, Angry Birds, Super Mario; totally frustrated he thought, he just wanted to dig up some more dead bodies.

 Quiz night, that night, Alfie Richardson was not feeling well. He had the quiz all prepared, so Annie rang Jimmy, and asked him if he would run the quiz. Jimmy was ecstatic, this could be the big breakthrough for James Moran, he thought. It went okay; Jimmy did his best. The card school put a team in with Julian Jameson's new neighbour Ray Titcombe. They unfortunately did not win, but they all agreed they were looking forward to next Tuesday's card school, back up to four members.

DI Judd, DS Roach and DC Brentwood had their work cut out that day, and the next day, obtaining statements from the two darts teams and locals at Ye Olde Elm Tree. The statements were almost identical. The dart threw itself! DI Judd thought Detective Chief Superintendent Thackeray was not going to be pleased with the outcome of these statements.

Friday, George started another dig in a random area. This proved to be ineffective. The lab results came back for the second grave, consisting of a male, average height, five foot nine, five to ten years younger than the first body recovered. The police and the archaeologists decided to secure the site for the weekend.

The Chen family arrived at 3 pm on the Friday. It was pandemonium for Annie at first. She wanted to put Ju and Liling in the bedroom with the two single beds, on the top floor. Fan and Gang being boyish, did not want to sleep together in the double bed on the top floor. There was much discussion, before eventually Ju and Liling agreed to sleep together in the double bed. Much to Annie's dismay, the negotiation continued. Young Lan and Huang could not share a room, so Mrs Chen offered to share a room with daughter Lan, and Mr Chen would share a room with son Huang. Annie escorted them all to their respective rooms.

Afterwards she strolled back down to the bar and thought, I need a holiday!

That night was humid; Ju and Liling had their window open, as did Fan and Gang on the top floor. Both windows were ajar. It was approximately 2 am when both windows flew open, consecutively. The two brothers remained asleep and never discovered the open window until the next morning. The window flying open woke Liling. She got out of bed and tried to close it. It was as if a force was stopping her. She glared out of the window in her sleepy state, and thought she saw something move in the garden, but went back to bed.

Mary came in early on the Saturday morning to help Annie with the breakfasts. When Annie telephoned Mrs Chen in the week, she enquired over their choice of food. Annie laid on buns stuffed with meat, and spicy pancakes with eggs. The breakfasts were well received, and the Chen family confirmed, same again tomorrow morning would suffice. Annie was relieved, no incidents last night. She was unaware about the windows in the top bedrooms.

Saturday morning, Ernie arrived with Annie's emergency beer order.

'You are mega busy Annie, what's the latest gossip?' asked Ernie. Annie gave Ernie the run down, the second grave, another skeleton dug up, a search for a third possible grave was underway. Annie confided in Ernie; it was his cheerful, cheeky disposition that she liked.

Nick Fitzsimons called on Farmer Granville Warren to try and establish the cost of repairs to his and Annie's fences. The two men took a stroll over to the area concerned. Granville offered to repair both fences and bill the reporter. Nick agreed and gave Granville his business card, with his details.

'What made you do it?' asked Granville.

'I thought I might get a few decent photographs of the archaeological excavation; I thought at night would be excellent timing,' he replied. Nick then went into graphic detail about his encounter with the birds; and the two shadows that disappeared; he became agitated as he described what happened. Granville heard his story, and put his arm around Nick's shoulder to comfort him.

'That must have been terrible,' Granville replied. As they parted company, Granville shook his head and thought, the man's a nutcase!

The Chen family had a great day out climbing, walking and, sight-seeing; they were all exhausted. A couple of drinks in the bar and early to bed. On Saturday night the weather had changed. A rolling mist from the nearby hillside was engulfing Ye Olde Elm Tree. Very few visitors that night. Granville and Farmer Forde were having a heated debate about government farm subsidies. Annie listened on and thought she was glad she was not in farming. Annie closed the bar promptly at 11 pm.

At a similar time to the previous night, Liling and Ju's bedroom window flew open. Simultaneously, Fan and Gang's window opened fully. The mist rolled into both rooms. It was more like a fog than a mist. It quickly filled the rooms. It was thick, like smoke; visibility in each room was rapidly getting worse. The mist was damp, soaking, wet. Ju in her sleep, brushed her hair, it was soaking wet. She woke, startled, fumbled for her glasses and the bedside lamp.

"Oh, my goodness" she yelled, waking her sister. The two girls panicked; they both leapt out of bed. Liling tried to close the window, as she did the previous night, but it was stuck, and she could not move it. The mist seemed to be rolling in the room, faster, thicker, dense. There was a strong musty, damp, rotting smell, in the air. The two ladies ran out of their room with fright, then banged on their brothers' bedroom door. The mist followed them into the corridor. Gang jumped out of bed, and switched the light on; he could hardly see the wardrobes at the far end of the room, the mist, fog, was so intense. Gang tried to close his bedroom window. It would not budge. This is crazy he thought. The two brothers opened their bedroom door to join their sisters. The mist had filled the corridor. There were two windows on the corridor leading to the front of the property; Gang tried to open them, but they were stuck too. They all carefully felt their way downstairs, where Annie and Mr and Mrs Chen had been woken by the commotion. The mist had reached their floor.

'You need to close your bedroom windows,' shouted Annie.

'We tried,' exclaimed Gang, 'The windows were stuck, I could not move them.'

Annie ran upstairs, ran into the brothers' bedroom, and closed the window with ease. Next room, again she closed the window unrestrained. She looked around the room; the bedcovers, chair cushions, dressing table, everything was soaking wet.

CHAPTER 23 – THE STORM

The next morning, at the family's request, Annie prepared the same breakfast for the Chen Family. The conversation throughout breakfast was the incredible happening of the night before. The family cornered Mary; they wanted her to hear every detail. Mary was flabbergasted.

Detective Constable Liz Brentwood telephoned Detective Inspector Judd on her mobile phone. She announced there were only two more Burton Arms dart players to contact and obtain statements. The Inspector was concerned that this process had been long-drawn-out, presenting no conclusive evidence. DC Brentwood had also telephoned the hospital; they were pleased with Ruben Hagen's progress. Good news at last, thought the inspector.

Shortly after the Chen family had checked out, Annie took a call from Charles Braithwaite. He wanted to hear Annie's explanation on what happened on the darts night.

'Their captain was showing off Charles,' added Annie, 'He was being provocative and irritating. He paraded around the pub affronting locals and Ye Olde Elm Tree players. Not sure who threw the dart at him? I didn't see it being thrown, but it was hell of a good shot,' declared Annie. Charles was astonished at Annie's comments; not what he was expecting to hear. He would have to improve on the story for his board of directors.

On Sunday morning, Brigit came to collect the laundry. Annie was often amused by her appearance; curly dark hair, almost orange make-up, and a silver jumpsuit. Brigit commented on how wet all the bedding was. Annie decided not to try and pass comment; only to say, how the windows had been left open and the mist had got in the two bedrooms.

Sunday lunchtime was buzzing with tourists and onlookers. Sunday evening was slightly less frenetic. Bob Truman came in for a couple of pints. Annie explained about the two top floor windows, both jammed open for the Chen family. Bob promised to pop by next day and check them out.

Monday morning, cellar duties. Annie was just about to start her chores when she checked the diary for the weekend ahead. There was a Polish, Gronowski family, staying at the inn. Annie has allocated them two rooms on her floor. An Italian couple, Luigi Bianchi and Lauretta Mancini, are booked into the top floor, double room. No one in the Toby Devons' room she thought; that might be just as well. An hour into her cellar work, the telephone rang. It was an Evie Grealish on the line, looking for a room for the Friday and Saturday. There was an air of reluctance with Annie to give the last room away, then her head started to rule her heart. She welcomed the income and took the booking. She jotted the details in the pub diary and put the phone down to Evie Grealish, except it was not Evie, it was Catheryn Devons.

Detective Sergeant Roach and contractor George arrived almost together on the Monday morning. George suggested to dig closer to the two graves, now that the archaeologists have finished their work on site. DS Roach agreed. George lit a cigarette and fired up his mini digger. Let us go find a body or two he said to himself.

Bob Truman came by to inspect the top floor bedroom windows.

'Sorry Annie, but they are both opening and closing perfectly well,' said Bob, 'I couldn't find anything wrong with them.' Annie thanked him for having a look; she looked confused.

DS Roach stood over two new grave-sized holes in the pub garden that George had created. He telephoned DI Judd from his mobile with no news, on that day's dig. The Inspector informed the Sergeant that they should close-down the operation at Ye Old Elm Tree for most of the week as there is a very severe storm, which the Met Office have named **Edna**. It is forecast to hit the coastline late afternoon on the Tuesday. The sergeant broke the news to George, he was gutted.

On the Tuesday lunchtime Annie had noticed how trade had dropped off. She looked out of her pub window and saw the wind was getting stronger.

'Looks like that storm Edna is well on its way,' she said to Mollie. 'I went to let Chester out of the back door just now; he was not amused; he wouldn't venture outside at first.'

Detective Chief Superintendent Raj Thackeray received a telephone call from Donald Rutherford SC, Senior Counsel.

'Good day sir,' said the barrister. 'I have had several conversations with your Detective Inspector Judd concerning the disappearance of the three, then four gentlemen, at Ye Olde Elm Tree public house and inn. The time lag for answers, even a conclusion, worry me somewhat Superintendent, do you have any progress that you can enlighten me with?' he asked. It was noticeable that the barrister had targeted DI Judd's superior, attempting to achieve further clarification on the investigation. The Superintendent tried to placate the barrister with an update on more excavations planned, the hindrance of the archaeological findings, and now storm Edna has unfortunately delayed progress.

'Ah yes, Edna,' replied the barrister in a sarcastic manner. 'I'll have to inform the families of Aylott, Foreman, Hardwick and McLarty about storm Edna, I am sure that will help their anxiety.' That telephone call exasperated the Superintendent. If only he could increase resources on the investigation. Time perhaps to move DI Judd to another assignment; someone needs to be held responsible.

On the Tuesday evening the wind was howling, and the rain was driving almost sideways. Farmer Forde was the only customer in Ye Olde Elm Tree until the card school arrived. Apart from catching up on events with the newspaper, he had a heart to heart conversation with Annie; the dart incident, the break-in to the garden, the accidents, the murder. The card school looked soaking wet when they entered the pub.

'You lot looked soaked,' declared Annie.

'We've only come from the car park,' claimed Jules. The new team member, Ray Titcombe, offered to drive everyone to the pub. He had asked Annie to stock a few bottles of zero alcohol beers.

'Fair play Ray, for drinking that nonsense,' said Norm. The card school left earlier than normal because of the weather. Annie closed the pub early that night.

Annie had a restless night. She was listening to the rain pounding on her bedroom window; it seemed to come in waves with the gusts of wind. She was alone in the pub, which never normally fazed her but that night the footsteps on the corridor were there to be heard. She was up early and telephoned Mary.

'No need to come to the pub today Mary,' said Annie, 'There were very few people in the pub yesterday, thanks to this atrocious weather. Take the day off, we will see you Thursday.' Mary gratefully accepted Annie's offer, not wanting to venture out in the storm.

On the Wednesday evening, the darts team were scheduled for an away match with the Red Lion. Landlord Bill telephoned Annie suggesting they should cancel; they both agreed. Annie's next task would be to contact all the pub's dart players with the news.

By the Wednesday evening, Annie watched the local news on the television. There was a great deal of localised flooding. In nearby Calamity Creek, as the locals referred to it, the emergency services were evacuating people from their homes. There were reports of both telephone and power lines down. Annie picked up her telephone landline, it was dead. Only the two farmers ventured out for a pint that night. They will be ok, thought Annie, they both drive four-wheel drive vehicles. Another early to bed evening for Annie, the wind and rain still prominent. Annie listened for footsteps, before she eventually dropped off to sleep. None to be heard, but there was a strong mildew, mouldy, fusty smell of damp. A smell she had never experienced before, in her bedroom.

By Thursday morning, Edna had moved inland and was causing havoc to other areas of the countryside. Annie ventured downstairs into the kitchen area.

'Chester, you have to go in the garden to do your business,' said Annie. The dog had a definite frown. Annie put on her wellington boots; everywhere looked sodden. Chester barked and ran over to the bottom corner of the garden. Annie could see from the pub that there had been a form of a landslide. Part of Annie's garden had finished up in Granville's farmland. Chester continued to bark. Annie waded over to the bottom of the garden; it was extremely muddy and squelchy. As she reached the far corner, Chester stopped barking. To Annie's amazement the landslide had exposed the top of two grave headstones; one was an upright headstone, the other was in the form of a cross.

CHAPTER 24 – UNWANTED VISITORS

That morning, Annie telephoned Detective inspector Judd with the news of the storm damage and landslide, exposing two newly discovered grave headstones. The Inspector thanked Annie for letting her know. She would try and round up Dr Bell and try and jointly visit Ye Olde Elm Tree later that morning. The inspector telephoned Doctor Cynthia Bell. The doctor was ecstatic with the news. They agreed to meet at Ye Olde Elm Tree at 10 am. As DI Judd left the office she swung by her Superintendent's office with the news.

'Are you surprised Rita?' asked Detective Chief Superintendent Raj Thackeray.

'Nothing surprises me any more with that old public house, sir' she replied.

Charles Braithwaite's first task of the day was to email his board of directors with an update on Ye Olde Elm Tree. He started by saying there was an incident soon to be in the media, concerning two of his public houses. Ye Olde Elm Tree hosting the league darts match and the visitors, the Burton Arms. Charles did not mention the alleged behaviour of the Burton Arms captain, just that he threw final darts at the board, after winning his game, at the end of match; one dart seemingly bounced off the board and into his eye. The gentleman is currently in hospital recovering, the police are gathering statements from all the players of both teams, but no foul play was suspected. Charles read the email several times before he finally pressed. Send.

10 am, Dr Bell and DI Judd met up at Ye Olde Elm Tree. Annie walked them down to the far corner of the garden. The ground was like a quagmire.

'That certainly was a horrendous storm over the last few days,' declared the Inspector. 'There are reports from all over the County of damage and localised flooding.'

'It has provided a considerable favour to us, exposing what could be a new historic site, perhaps even a heritage site,' commented Dr Bell. The three all agreed that to start any further excavation could be days away following the devastation of storm Edna. They thanked Annie and walked back to their vehicles.

'It will be necessary now to involve the County Council, Rita' said Dr Bell. 'This could result in change of ownership on the entire site, including the public house.' DI Judd promised to talk to the County Council next.

Pub company director Douglas Winterbottom read Charles Braithwaite's email and smiled. This could be kudos for him and the company, with the daily newspaper. He telephoned his good friend, the editor of the Star News, Colin Coombes. The two men agreed to send a reporter and a photographer along to the hospital to get a story and a few photographs. Colin Coombes would need to know who the darts captain of the Burton Arms was.

'Leave it with me,' said Douglas Winterbottom.

Charles Braithwaite received a telephone call from his director Douglas Winterbottom.

'Charles, be a good chap and get me the Burton Arms' dart team captain's name,' asked Douglas. 'I am arranging a surprise visit for him, at the hospital, from the daily tabloid.'

Douglas hung up the phone and grinned to himself. Charles put the phone down, wearing a somewhat bemused expression.

Late Thursday afternoon, Annie took a call from Alfie Richardson, the quiz master for that evening. He had all the quiz arranged but he still felt dreadful and wouldn't be capable of hosting the quiz that evening; he asked Annie if she could cover him? Annie put the phone down thinking Alfie did not sound very well. She phoned Jimmy, who jumped at the chance to help out, once again. The night after Edna, the pub was quite quiet, with just three teams. It did not run as smoothly as normal, but Jimmy enjoyed himself immensely.

DI Judd called back at the station. DCS Raj Thackeray noticed her return and called her into his office.

'How's the statements going from both dart teams?' he asked.

'Nothing conclusive sir,' she replied, 'Can you believe no one saw who threw the dart, most said it threw itself!'

'That is preposterous,' ranted the Superintendent. 'Who did the Burton Arms captain play against?' DI Judd took her notebook out of her top pocket, flicked a few pages.

'It was Ye Olde Elm Tree captain, a Charlie Hind, everyone refers to him as Chas,' she answered.

'Let's bring him in for questioning, after all, it sounds like he might have had a motive,' suggested the Superintendent.

'The charge Sir?' asked the Inspector.

'Grievous bodily harm of course, Rita,' DCS Thackeray answered, with not so much of a look in the direction of the Inspector. She left his office thinking her senior officer was sending her on a fool's errand.

Reporter Godfrey Wallace and photographer Eamon Fuller from the Star News newspaper arrived at the hospital. Ruben Hagen was in a private room, his eye covered by bandage. Godfrey explained who they represented. Ruben was only too pleased to unload his aggravation and annoyance regarding his eye injury. The pair left the hospital. Eamon had taken some good photographs of Ruben with his eye bandaged, he showed Godfrey from his camera.

'I have several photos of the Ye Olde Elm Tree, none of the Burton Arms though. I could just drive over there and take a few in case you can use them,' said Eamon.

'This is going to make a great story,' said Godfrey, 'Poltergeist!'

Friday morning, the first guests arrived at Ye Olde Elm Tree. The Gronowski family. The daughter Lena spoke fluent English, so she handled the booking in process. Annie showed them to their rooms on the first floor. The two daughters seemed quite excited; Lena, sixteen and Lidia, fourteen.

DI Judd and DC Brentwood arrived at the home of Charlie Hind. His wife Yolanda answered the door, with a small child in her arms. The inspector was very diplomatic, suggesting that she had a question she would like to ask Charlie, concerning the dart incident. Yolanda explained that Charlie worked at a local bakery and would be home at about 5 pm. The officer thanked her and returned to the car. Yolanda closed the door and thought, that was odd.

Next to arrive that day at Ye Olde Elm Tree was Italian couple Luigi Bianchi and Lauretta Mancini. They cuddled as they booked in. Annie could not help but notice Luigi caressing Lauretta's posterior. Annie led them to their room on the top floor.

DCS Raj Thackeray made a phone call to his equivalent officer in the Greater Manchester Police Department. He enquired on a possible loan to his department of Detective Inspector Graeme Dankworth. Raj had been tracking the DI and was impressed with his CV. The Superintendent was told that DI Dankworth was about to conclude a missing person case and could possibly be loaned out, on a temporary basis, in the next few weeks. That was music to Raj Thackeray's ears.

Back at the station, DC Brentwood approached DI Judd's desk.

'Ma'am I have found out for you who is Head of Planning and Development for the County Council, it is a Mr Fitzroy Ebanks, here are his contact details.' The DC handed the Inspector a page from her notebook. The DI thanked her and proceeded to call Mr Ebanks to set up a meeting.

5 pm, 'Time to make another call on Charlie Hind, Liz,' said DI Judd.

The two officers drove to Chas Hind's house, he answered the door.

'Mr Hind,' announced DI Judd 'We are **arresting** you on suspicion of causing grievous bodily harm to Mr Ruben Hagen. You **do** not have to say anything, but it may harm your defence, if you **do** not mention when questioned, something which you later rely on **in** court. Anything you do say, may be given in evidence.' The detective constable cuffed Charlie Hind.

'I didn't touch the guy and I can prove it,' yelled Chas. His wife Yolanda came to the door to see what all the commotion was about.

'Where are you taking my husband?' shrieked Yolanda. Chas looked back at his wife as he was led to the police car, and called out,

'Don't worry darling, it is all a big misunderstanding, they think I threw the dart at the Burton Arms' captain. But it was not me, I was nowhere near him.'

6 pm, opening time, Annie wondered what time her next guest would arrive, under the name of Evie Grealish. Annie felt palpitations when Richard and Catheryn Devons walked through the pub front door.

'I am really sorry, but I am instructed by the police not to serve you,' Annie said in a quiet tone.

'We haven't come to be served,' replied Catheryn Devons, 'We have booked a room for two nights stay.'

'There must be some mistake,' replied Annie, 'We only have one room remaining for this weekend, and that is booked to a Ms Grealish.'

'Yes, that is me,' replied Catheryn, 'Evie Grealish.' Annie looked stunned.

'You booked under a false name! How dare you,' answered Annie. 'I am sorry but I cannot let you have that room, under the circumstances.' There was a pause.

'I'm sorry too, because you took my debit card details over the phone, I have already paid for the room,' replied Catheryn.

'No problem, I can refund you,' said Annie wittingly.

'Not if I don't offer you my debit card,' came a sarcastic answer.

Annie thought for a moment. Could she refund the couple in cash, she thought? Then she cussed; Annie went to the bank that day, she would not have enough cash in the till to credit a two-night stay, plus she only had a cash float in the pub safe. Annie started to look embarrassed, most of the people in the pub were listening in to the conversation, and the pub was quite busy.

'Follow me,' Annie said grudgingly, 'I will show you to your room, it is on the top floor.' The couple followed Annie up the first flight of stairs. Catheryn noticed a wooden sign on one of the bedroom doors. On it was etched Annie's room. It was a joke Christmas present off Annie's late husband Bert. He always joked, calling her the boss of their relationship, so he figured their bedroom should be called Annie's room. Annie led them up a second flight of stairs and showed them into their room. Richard walked over to the window, studied the garden below and said,

'This will do nicely, thank you.' Annie was not comfortable with this arrangement.

It was a busy evening in Ye Olde Elm Tree, lots of locals as well as some inquisitive tourists. Farmer Forde, Granville, Monica, Desmond People and Alice. Eddie and Barbara in the snug; guests Luigi and Lauretta were also in the snug, and to Annie's annoyance, so were Richard and Catheryn Devons. Dart player Terry Thornley came in with the news that darts captain Chas had been arrested for throwing the dart into the Burton Arms' captain's eye. Annie was astounded with this news.

'He was stood at the bar waiting to be served, nowhere near the dartboard,' declared Annie. Terry tended to agree with her.

'Yes, now you come to mention it, I think you are right, Annie.'

Annie went into the back room, and decided to call DI Judd on her mobile.

'Hello Inspector, it's Annie Baines from Ye Olde Elm Tree.' DI Judd became suddenly uneasy; what is happening now she thought. Annie explained how Charlie Hind was stood at the bar waiting to be served and nowhere near the dart board when the accident happened. She also told the Inspector how she had been tricked by a false name and Richard Devons and his wife were staying at Ye Olde Elm Tree for two nights. DI Judd put the phone down, and wished for no further incidents with the Devons couple. She then telephoned the station and instructed the release of Charlie Hlnd. Annie's statement matched Charlie Hind's declaration.

Richard and Catheryn were sat at the next table to Eddie and Barbara. It seemed as if the couple were eavesdropping on their conversation; Barbara started to feel agitated. She leaned over to Eddie and whispered in his ear,

'Let's move on to another pub for a final drink.' Eddie agreed and the couple shortly left. Richard and Catheryn drank in Ye Olde Elm Tree all evening. They were quite inebriated by the time it was last orders and time for bed.

In the middle of the night, Catheryn Devons woke to the sound of voices reciting. She went to look out of her bedroom window; she had no idea it was the same window that Toby Devons had fallen from. As she stared down into the garden, the chanting seemed to have stopped. At the bottom of the garden by the big tree, it looked like five or six figures, shadows like silhouettes standing in a group, huddled together, motionless. She dismissed it and sat back on the bed. Richard was fast asleep. She kept thinking of the sign on the door, downstairs, Annie's room. She was feeling mischievous; could she play a prank on the landlady, by entering her room in the middle of the night? There was a half-bottle of wine on her bedside table. She soon polished off the wine, plotting ways to possibly frighten landlady Annie Baines.

Catheryn crept downstairs and stood outside Annie's room. She waited a few minutes, grabbed the door handle, and tried to prize the bedroom door open. It was latched from the inside. The noise woke Annie; she was startled, what the hell was that? she incoherently thought. Catheryn tried to open the door again, and again, in temper. Annie soon realised someone was trying to break into her room.

She heard an "aargh," desperation sound; sounded like Catheryn Devons she thought. Catheryn gave up, turned around, when it was as if a hand had clamped down upon her shoulder, followed by a strong push in the centre of her back. Catheryn fell down a flight of stairs, with an almighty crash. She lay motionless at the bottom of the stairs, her head resting awkwardly on the bottom bannister, her arm twisted beneath her. Annie never moved, she stayed rooted to her bed. She feared whoever it was, they had fallen down the stairs.

It was Mr Gronowski who appeared first. He fumbled along the landing wall in search of a light switch. Eventually he turned the light on to see a crumpled female body at the bottom of the stairs. His two daughters opened their bedroom door; Lidia gave out a scream. Mrs Gronowski ventured onto the corridor. She put her hands over her face in anguish, and shooed her daughters back into their room. Mr Gronowski noticed for the first time; Annie's room sign on the bedroom door. He knocked on the door.

'Hello is there anyone there,' he said in his strong Polish accent. Annie unlatched the door, with a clunk, and stepped into the passage.

'There is a lady at the bottom of the stairs,' exclaimed Mr Gronowski, 'She has fallen down the stairs!' Annie walked over to the top of the stairs where she could see it was Catheryn Devons.

'Oh, my goodness,' sighed Annie, 'What was she doing walking around in the dark, in the middle of the night, poor girl.' Mr Gronowski looked confused.

'I will telephone the emergency services,' said Annie, as she ran down to her living quarters to phone 999, for both an ambulance and for the police. Her next move was to venture up to the top floor to inform Richard Devons. He was oblivious to what had just happened, snoring, in a deep sleep.

Annie shook his arm, 'Mr Devons,' she called, as she tried to wake him. Richard woke alarmingly. 'Mr Devons, your wife, in the dark, has just fallen down the stairs. I have phoned for an ambulance,' said Annie, as calmly as she could.

Richard Devons opened his eyes wide, he glared at Annie. If looks could kill!

CHAPTER 25 – THE HEADSTONES

Richard Devons quickly dressed in shorts and t-shirt and raced down two flights of stairs, to his beloved Catheryn. She seemed unconscious, but she was breathing. Her head did look very awkwardly placed.

'I would not try and move her, Mr Devons,' suggested Annie, 'I would wait for the emergency services to arrive; they will be here soon.'

Richard sat on the bottom of the stairs, holding Catheryn's hand. His eyes filled. The first to arrive were the police. Annie met them at the front door of the pub. On duty that night were Detective Inspector Maurice Lawson and Detective Constable Anish Tamun; they introduced themselves to the landlady.

'I am the Licensee here, Annie Baines,' she said.

'Yes, we know who you are,' replied the Detective Inspector, 'It seems you have been in the news quite extensively in recent weeks,' he smiled. Annie took them through to the staircase where Catheryn was laying. The DI asked how it happened? Annie answered,

'Mr & Mrs Devons were drinking all evening in our snug; it would appear the young lady must have fallen down the stairs in the dark.' Richard rose to his feet. He glared at Annie,

'Don't you mean she was pushed!' he claimed, 'By you!' he pointed his finger at Annie. At that moment, the ambulance arrived and took the heat out of the situation.

The paramedics were excellent, they were able to neck brace and sedate Catheryn and carry her off to the ambulance on a stretcher. Richard held Catheryn's hand and climbed into the ambulance with her. DI Lawson went through the guest list with Annie.

'Gronowski family?' he asked. Annie pointed out how they were staying on the first floor. She detailed the rooms in which they were staying, and pointed out that Mr Gronowski was first to the scene.

'A Mr Bianchi and Mrs Mancini,' the DI continued.

'They are on the top floor, possibly having slept through it all,' answered Annie. The Detective Inspector asked DC Tamun to check on the couple upstairs.

'And finally, Evie Grealish. Was that Evie that had fallen down the stairs?' asked the Inspector. Annie stuttered,

'No, she booked in as Evie Grealish, but she is actually Catheryn Devons and that was her husband Richard that wrongly accused me earlier.'

'Devons?' enquired DI Lawson, 'It was a Devons brothers' cousin, that died here recently wasn't it?" he asked. Annie looked solemn.

'There have been three Devons accidents,' was her reply, 'A lean-to fell on a Garrett Devons, a Gresham Devons was killed with a garden fork, and a Toby Devons fell out of a bedroom window.' She shook her head in anguish.

'And now the lady found injured at the bottom of your stairs makes four Devons!' the Inspector jeered. 'I will enjoy handing this case over to Detective Inspector Rita Judd on shift change in the morning,' mocked DI Lawson. With that the Inspector asked Annie outright, 'Mr Devons accused you of pushing her down the stairs?' Annie stammered,

'I was in my room; I always lock my door from the inside when we have guests. Mr Gronowski can vouch for that.' The Inspector wrote Annie's answer in his notebook and underlined it several times. Annie refrained from telling the Inspector how Catheryn Devons had tried to break into her room. DC Tamun reappeared from the top floor; he confirmed that the Italian guests upstairs had not heard or seen anything.

Annie did not go back to bed, her guests did, but she was wide awake, very conscious. She decided to take Chester for a walk across the fields, dawn was breaking; the dog sensed this was abnormal. Mary arrived to see Annie staring at a cup of tea.

'Bad night?' asked Mary.

Annie explained how the Devons couple had checked in under a false name, how they were blind drunk when they went to bed, how Catheryn Devons had tried to break into her room, in the middle of the night, and how she had fallen down the stairs and was badly injured. How Annie had to call out the emergency services once again, which was followed by police interrogation. Mary consoled Annie with a hug; she then produced a copy of the Star News.

'I'm afraid, Annie, you are front page news once more,' announced Mary.

Annie looked at the front of newspaper and tried to hide the tears. The headline read 'DART CAPTAIN BLINDED BY A DART IN HIS EYE.' There were photographs of a bandaged Ruben Hagen in hospital and both the Burton Arms and Ye Olde Elm Tree. The report was quite damning that someone or something had thrown the dart; the insinuation was a poltergeist at Ye Olde Elm Tree.

'What else could it be?' Annie asked, having read the article.

Mary had an idea, 'Why don't we hold a séance or better still, get a priest to exorcise the pub?'

Annie replied, 'I'm not sure that is a wise thing to do.'

Mary started to clean the kitchen sink. She turned and said, 'My Bryan knows a spiritualist. He says people that have connected with her have spoken very highly of her.' Annie still was not sure. Mary promised to ask Bryan for more information.

Di Judd was in the office catching up on emails when DI Lawson walked in, on shift change, with a big grin on his face.

'What's the smirk for Maurice?' asked DI Judd, 'Another lazy nightshift with no police work?'

'Quite the contrary Rita,' replied DI Lawson, 'A busy night with emergency services. This poor female fell down a flight of stairs and injured herself quite badly. It all took place in a public house.' DI Lawson had the Inspector's undivided attention.

'Yes, it was in a public house called Ye Olde Elm Tree, and her name was,' DI Lawson fumbled through his notepad for effect, 'Devons, that's right, Devons, Catheryn Devons,' he added. DI Judd looked stunned when she suddenly realised,

'You had me going there for a minute Maurice, one of your little practical jokes,' she proclaimed.

'No joke Rita.' Di Lawson pulled up a chair next to her desk and referred to his notes. 'Catheryn Devons; her husband Richard travelled in the ambulance to the hospital with her. Landlady, Mrs Baines, was somewhat aloof about what had happened, claimed Catheryn had been drinking all evening and swore she was in her room with the door latched? Worth investigating further Rita. There was an Italian couple upstairs, seemed to sleep through it all. There was a Gronowski family on the first floor and Mrs Baines was adamant, Mr Gronowski was the first on the scene, implying that if anyone pushed her down the stairs, it was him, so definitely worth interviewing him.' DI Judd shook her head with incredulity.

'Thank you very much for all that Maurice,' said DI Judd, "You can bugger off now!' the DI was joking but irritated.

It was the weekend. Charles Braithwaite took a wander down to his local shops. He entered the newsagents and spotted a photograph of Ye Olde Elm Tree on the front page of the Star News. He picked up the tabloid and read the headlines 'DART CAPTAIN BLINDED ...' He read the report with intrigue. The report finished with a strong emphasis that a poltergeist was responsible. That was not quite how Charles would like to present the accident to his board of directors; he would add some ambiguity.

The early prognosis on Catheryn Devons was a cervical fracture of several vertebrae bones that made up the spine in the neck, a dislocated shoulder, and a fracture of her right forearm with both the radius and the ulna bones fractured. Catheryn was heavily sedated in a semi-conscious state. The hospital was the first location DI Judd visited that morning. She did manage to ascertain that Catheryn was pushed down the stairs, she did not see who pushed her, plus she had tried to break into the landlady's bedroom, for a joke, but it was locked. DI Judd asked to meet with the senior consultant at the hospital. The Inspector requested a private room so that Richard could stay with his wife overnight. She had to explain the reasons why; she did not want Richard Devons returning to Ye Olde Elm Tree, to stay a second night.

DI Judd's next call was to see Annie at Ye Olde Elm Tree. Annie gave her description of events, which transpired to be quite similar to her recollection, she had given DI Lawson earlier.

'One thing is confusing me Mrs Baines,' said the Inspector, 'You haven't mentioned what Catheryn Devons told me earlier; Catheryn, tried to break into your room!' DI Judd waited for an answer.

'Yes,' said Annie, 'She tried several times. I have no idea what she wanted. My door was latched, I latch it every night, especially when we have guests. The last person to try and enter my room in the middle of the night was Toby Devons.'

'Did you open your door, to either Catheryn or Toby?' came the probing question.

'No, I was unsure what she, or Toby, wanted in the middle of the night. To be honest I was scared, on both occasions and quite rightly so with Toby, who had an axe in his room. With Catheryn, I heard a crash; I suspected she had fallen down the stairs, but I just froze, I couldn't move,' continued Annie.

DI Judd then asked if she could see Mr and Mrs Gronowski. Annie set up a meeting with the family and the inspector in the snug. Mr Gronowski admitted to hearing someone trying to forcefully enter one of the bedrooms, it had woken him. He admitted to hearing a crash, that was when he decided to investigate what had happened. He confirmed there was no one else on the landing, he had to knock for Mrs Baines the landlady. The DI suspected that Annie might have pushed Catheryn down the stairs, re-entered her room and locked the door, however, there was no evidence, unless there might be DNA evidence on Catheryn's clothing? DI Judd decided she should call back into the hospital, and collect whatever Catheryn was wearing at the time.

DI Judd enquired about the Italian couple. They were still in bed; they had even missed breakfast. The Inspector thought she would catch up with them later, if necessary.

It was lunchtime trading when Richard Devons returned to Ye Olde Elm Tree to check out and collect his and Catheryn's belongings.

Annie asked Richard, rather sheepishly, 'How is your wife?'

'Broken neck, busted shoulder, broken arm, thanks,' came his reply. He ventured upstairs to the bedroom. Richard and Catheryn each had sports bags which he hurriedly repacked. On checking out, Annie gave Richard a full cash refund from current takings. She explained that they did not take breakfast, plus she felt she could not charge them for the room. Richard received the cash, looking down at the ground. He looked up; his eyes met Annie's eyes with a glare. He never thanked her, just turned around and walked out the front door. That made Annie feel, uncomfortable.

Company Director Douglas Winterbottom had read the front-page report on the dart incident at Ye Olde Elm Tree. He rang Charles Braithwaite at his home.

'Charles dear chap, what do you make of this poltergeist suggestion in the Star News?' he asked.

'Sir, I would not read too much into it, these tabloid newspapers are always looking for a story out of the ordinary,' came his cautious reply.

'Stay close to it Charles, if it can be proven the old place is haunted, we could advertise the fact, increase the visitors and possibly put up the rent!' came the Directors reply.

'Yes sir, good idea, I will follow up on it,' answered Charles.

On the Monday morning just as Annie was about to start her cellar work, she looked out of the pub window and thought to herself, here are the cavalry. Contractor George Pullman with his mini digger loaded on his truck, Detective Sergeant Roach, and Doctors Bell, Donnelly, and Bunce, had all arrived. The three doctors discussed and agreed their priority for the day ahead; to expose the two headstones to see what they could learn.

Detective Chief Superintendent Raj Thackeray took a telephone call from Greater Manchester Police. Detective Inspector Graeme Dankworth could possibly be available the following week to assist with Raj Thackeray's assignments. The DCS thought of making an announcement to the media by the end of the week. He would have to try and time it well; when to inform Detective Inspector Rita Judd would be crucial.

DI Judd arrived at the County Council offices. A helpful receptionist led the police officer to the office of the Head of Planning and Development, Mr Fitzroy Ebanks. The councillor welcomed the Inspector and arranged for a pot of tea, to share.

'Ebanks is an unusual surname?' enquired DI Judd.

'Yes, I come from a large Ebanks family, from the Cayman Islands, in the Caribbean. Ebanks is quite a common name there. My parents moved to the UK when I was a small child. They sent me to a private school, I joined the civil service straight from school, and here I am. How can I help you Inspector?' came his reply.

The Inspector explained that she wanted to talk to him regarding Ye Olde Elm Tree. Fitzroy Ebanks knew all about recent events at the pub from the television and newspapers. He was unaware of the two new headstones revealed by storm Edna. They discussed the possibility of a change of land and property ownership and set a date to meet at Ye Olde Elm Tree.

Chas Hind set off for work at the bakery that morning, glad to be home with his wife and family. They discussed over breakfast whether Chas should visit Ruben Hagen in the hospital after work. Chas was not keen on the idea, but felt he should try and show some sympathy.

That afternoon, Mary telephoned Annie with news of the séance. She had spoken to her boyfriend Bryan and had the contact details of a medium.

'Her professional name is Madame Holz,' said Mary, 'All you need is seven to attend; we could use that big round table in your snug.' Annie thought about it for a second.

'Why seven?' she asked.

'Glad you asked me that Annie. I asked Bryan the same question. I had to write down his answer, it's far too complicated,' replied Mary. She continued to explain,

'You should mix people indiscriminately, around the table, male, female or by profession. There are seven spheres to the astral plane, or seven layers of heaven. The spheres are invisible to each other. No space between spheres. It is perceived that the first few spheres are where spirits can reside, happily, conduct prayers, attend churches. Mediums can exist on the first sphere. Invisible forces can come down from the higher spheres to teach the spirits. Escalation through the spheres depend solely on the desire of the spirit to move on. Some spirits are reluctant to move on at all. Other spirts may wait for a loved one to join them, or a problem to be resolved. Bryan explained it as, imagine it like a whirlpool looking down on our world.' Annie did not answer at first.

'Mary you have just spooked me to hell, I shall probably have nightmares tonight now,' Annie responded anxiously.

'I reckon we can easily get seven together Annie,' construed Mary, 'You, me, Bryan, the medium, I bet Brigit who does the laundry would join us, only need another two more to hold a séance. Maybe another male participant? Shall I go ahead and arrange it?' Mary asked.

'Yes, I suppose so, something has to change around here,' replied Annie.

Annie checked the diary for the forthcoming weekend. Two couples from the Netherlands had booked to stay, due to arrive on the Thursday lunchtime. A Mr De Vries and Ms Bakker, a Mr Derwater and Ms Timmermans. Annie had booked them all into first floor rooms. No one in the loft rooms, thank goodness, she murmured to herself.

Chas Hind visited Ruben Hagen in hospital. Ruben was quite pleased to see his visitor. He had a copy of the Star News on his bedside table which he let Chas read.

'Do you believe a ghost may have thrown the dart?' he asked Ruben. The German shook his head; he did not believe in supernatural manifestations.

By the early evening, the archaeological excavation had reached a breaking point. The cross gravestone was badly corroded, the inscription was unreadable. The upright gravestone was enlightening. A name Theo 'kins. There was a verse exposed which closed 'short illness.' Then a date XX60 – 1902. The Doctors all agreed XX60 was undoubtably 1860. The man had died aged approximately forty-two. They had a year of his death, 1902, which may enable them to trace his death records. This was also a similar age to the first two bodies exhumed. His surname ending 'kins was a mystery.

The three doctors sat at the graveside testing each other's knowledge on names. They came up with thirteen possibilities. Simpkins, Hawkins, Dawkins, Atkins, Tomkins, Dickins, Jenkins, Johnkins, Perkins, Parkins, Watkins, Hopkins, Bodkins. There was a debate over the latter name, whether it was a real name. DS Roach thought this was highly amusing and wrote down the suggestions. He showed the list to Annie. She was curious and asked him, could she take a copy of the names? He handed Annie the list of names.

The conclusion for the next day was not to exhume the 'Theo' grave yet, but to focus on the grave with the cross headstone, in the bottom corner of the garden. They all agreed to meet at 9 am the next day.

It was 10.30 pm that evening when the pub telephone rang. Annie felt uneasy to answer it; something wrong she thought, a telephone call this late.

'Hello Annie, it's Mary,' said the caller.

'Mary why ever are you ringing me, so late in the evening?' Annie asked, 'We will see each other first thing in the morning.'

'Sorry Annie,'" came the reply, 'I was so excited, I had to ring you, I have fixed up the séance for this Thursday evening. Madame Holz plans to travel to the Czech Republic for the following two weeks, so it was our best chance to book her. All we need is another three members to make up the seven.' Annie put the phone down, wearing a scornful expression, not sure what she was letting herself in for?

CHAPTER 26 – THE SÉANCE

The cavalry, as Annie calls them, arrived at Ye Olde Elm Tree, punctually at 9 am. Doctors Bell, Donnelly, and Bunce, plus contractor George. Detective Sergeant Roach could not join them first thing, as he and Detective Inspector Judd were called to a domestic argument in a nearby town; a woman had stabbed her husband. The archaeological team had covered over and secured the grave of Theo. They started to excavate the grave with the cross headstone. George's mini digger had excavated approximately one metre, however the three doctors wanted to manually excavate, thereon. This did frustrate George.

Charles Braithwaite decided to drop by Ye Olde Elm Tree that morning. They had a short discussion on the Star News feature. Charles questioned Annie on the poltergeist theory.

'Well Charles, there are many rumours that this old pub is haunted. I am not surprised the newspaper reporter included it in his article,' Annie answered.

She was thankful that Charles had not heard yet of the Catheryn Devons tragic accident. Annie was somewhat bored of Charles' frequent visits, so she sent him into the garden to converse with the doctors. Dr Donnelly obliged Charles with an update; a forty-two, year old male, died 1902, named Theo, surname unknown, due to erosion of the headstone. Charles thanked the doctor. This was excellent information he could forward on to Douglas Winterbottom and his board of directors.

Winding up the excavation that day, the archaeological team had discovered two coffins laid side by side. An adult and a child. They all decided to secure the grave overnight and heft up the coffin lids in the morning.

Annie telephoned Brigit, who helps with the laundry each week. Annie approached the subject of the séance. Brigit apologised to Annie, as she was going on a blind date that night, otherwise she would have loved to sit in on a séance. Brigit had endless boyfriends over the years. She joked when Annie asked her,

'You never know Annie I might come across one of my ex-boyfriends up there floating on a cloud!' The two ladies laughed. Annie wished her good luck with her blind date.

That evening the card school met in Ye Olde Elm Tree. Jules Jameson had a small premium bond win, so he was offering to buy most of the drinks. Annie approached the subject of the séance with the card players. Jules was otherwise engaged with a local CAMRA (Campaign for Real Ale) monthly meeting on the Thursday. Badger declined as his wife was close to the birth of their third child. Ray Titcombe did not want to push his luck and ask his wife for a second night out, in a week, in the pub. Norman Prince, who happened to work for an undertaker, said yes, he would be happy to join in, he joked and said he might bump into a few of his recent clients.

Other regulars in the pub that evening, Monica, who said yes, (she saw it as an opportunity to possibly hear from her late husband Lawrence, who tragically lost his life at Ye Olde Elm Tree); estate agent Desmond People and his girlfriend

Alice. Annie approached the couple on the subject of the séance. For Desmond, he was not at all interested in participating. Alice was quite the reverse.

'Oh, I would love to partake in a real live séance,' she said.

'Are you sure?' questioned Desmond.

'Yes, it's something I have always wanted to do,' she replied. Annie had just signed up her seventh member of the circle.

The following day the exhumation was underway. Contractor George was stood down temporarily as the first task that morning was to lift the two coffin lids. The child's coffin looked the easier of the two, so they tackled that first. A young male, possible ten – twelve years old, with some deformity. The second coffin took much longer to open. Female, middle aged. Dr Bell implied that with the two bodies buried next to each other, it could possibly be mother and son. For the rest of the day the skeletal remains were exhumed for laboratory testing.

That evening it was the rearranged dart fixture at Ye Olde Elm Tree versus the Red Lion. The two teams elected to play seven a side. It was a close match, Ye Olde Elm Tree winning marginally, four–three; Captain Chas Hind winning the final game, to clinch the match for his team. There was very-little celebration after the ruckus of the previous home match. The following evening was to be the séance. Annie pondered on whether to carry on with the pre-booked quiz-night. Her conclusion was that they would take place in separate rooms so they should not clash, plus it could be another busy evening. She would ask both Mollie and Jimmy to work the bar that night.

The following day contractor George was stood down once more with the focus on the removal of the remaining bones from the two graves. There was further bad news for George, as on the Friday the area was to expect another severe storm. Normally the Meteorological Office would decide on the next storm's name. The last storm, Edna, was well remembered for the damage it caused. The Met Office would normally follow up with a boy's name beginning with the letter F. The storm about to arrive was on route to the UK from Spain, rather than from across the Atlantic Ocean. The storm had already been named by the Spanish Meteorological Office, **Emilio.**

Detective Inspector Judd took a telephone call from Detective Constable Liz Brentwood. There was no DNA match to Mrs Baines on the night t-shirt of Catheryn Devons.

'Thank you, Liz' said the Inspector. She ended the call and wondered who had pushed Catheryn down the stairs? Her husband Richard? But Annie had given him an alibi by racing upstairs to wake him? DI Judd drove off to meet Fitzroy Ebanks at Ye Olde Elm Tree.

Inspector Judd greeted Mr Ebanks as he arrived and parked in the pub car park. He was surprised at how busy the pub was. DI Judd took the Head of Planning into the public house to meet Annie, then she escorted him into the garden to meet the doctors and see the exhumation. Annie did wonder why the police were showing someone from the County Council the archaeological site. Dr Bell conducted the garden tour; the two late Victorian graves first found, and then the current exhumation. Fitzroy thanked the three doctors and walked back to his vehicle with the inspector.

'I can see the need for change of ownership,' said Fitzroy Ebanks, 'This would be a quite complex and uncommon application. It is likely to be a lengthy process.' The inspector agreed and thanked him for visiting Ye Olde Elm Tree.

Early that afternoon the two Dutch couples arrived at Ye Olde Elm Tree. Sem De Vries and Lotte Bakker signed the register first, followed by Luuk Derwater and Liv Timmermans. Liv asked Annie,

'How old is the inn?'

'It's reported to be over three hundred years old,' answered Annie.

'Is it haunted, does it have a ghost?' asked Lotte.

'Probably several ghosts,' joked Annie. All four guests looked at Annie inquisitively. 'I will show you to your rooms. After, if you like, there is an excavation in the back garden I can show you. There is a team of archaeologists working there; they have found a historic grave of a woman and child. Tonight, we have a séance organised in the small bar; a group of seven people hope to be speaking to the spirits.' The two ladies were enthralled by Annie's suggestions.

Alfie Richardson was setting up the quiz-night in the main bar when Madame Holz arrived at Ye Olde Elm Tree. She wore a black garment draped from head to toe. Annie asked her if she would like refreshment.

'Water,' was her reply. She insisted on walking around and around the snug to ascertain the venue's ambience. She embraced the large round table that Annie had assigned to hold the séance. She ran her black gloved hand over it several times. She then arranged the seven chairs with an equal distance apart.

First to arrive was Mary, with her new boyfriend Bryan. They walked into the snug and straight away Mary saw Madame Holz dressed in black and thought, she was exactly how she had imagined her from Bryan's description.

Next to arrive were Desmond People and Alice. They walked into the main bar to buy drinks. Jimmy served Desmond with a pint of scrumpy cider and Alice with her usual gin and tonic.

'Off you go then Alice and join your spiritual friends,' said Desmond in a joking manner.

'Aren't you going to join me?' she asked.

'No, I will have a chat at the bar, with Farmer Forde,' claimed Desmond.

'Only when I have finished reading from today's tabloid; Unsuccessful first dates,' said the Farmer, as he held up his newspaper to show them that was what he was genuinely reading. Alice ventured into the snug; she took one look at Madame Holz and became instantly nervous.

Card school Norman and Monica arrived simultaneously. Norman took his drink into the snug and watched Madame Holz setting up what looked like Tarot cards on the séance table. This is going to be fun he thought. Monica had different thoughts. Her late husband Lawrence, who was once Annie and Bert's gardener, was found face down in the pub's fishpond. She was hoping to make contact, with him that night.

The two Dutch couples were next to arrive. Annie explained to Madame Holz where they were from and that they were keen to attend, as observers. The medium ordered them to stand well away from the séance table, and to stand over by the door.

Madame Holz was ready to start the séance and asked her guests to be seated. It happened to coincide with the quiz-night starting; six teams that night. Annie raced into the main bar and asked Alfie Richardson to turn down his PA, as it could be heard in the other room. Madame Holz placed a Ouija Board in the centre of the table, indicating that they would use that later if there is no contact with the spirit world in the traditional way. The medium asked her audience to turn off their electrical devices, then the Spiritualist asked,

'Is there any one of you that would like to contact a friend, relative or loved one tonight?' Monica raised her arm.

'I lost my husband several years ago, he died here, at Ye Olde Elm Tree, he drowned in the fishpond. I wondered if he was still here, in spirit?'

'What was his name? Do you have a photograph?' asked Madame Holz.

'His name was Lawrence Boyd. Yes, I have a photo of him.' She reached into her purse and handed the medium a photograph.

'Let us begin,' said Madame Holz. 'Let us all hold hands to form a sphere of seven. She explained the three lit candles, on the table. Violet, to enhance psychic powers, blue, to enhance communication, orange to attract good things. Her audience looked impressed.

The medium began, 'We call out to the spirit world, guardian angels, to the spirit world, we mean you no harm. We claim, protection for everyone in the circle, and that no evil being can come near us. We seek the presence of Lawrence Boyd. Can you hear us Lawrence, can you show us a sign?' There was silence, no sign. Madame Holz swung her head violently to the left as if she had seen something move.

'I am receiving the letters BA. Does the name Armstrong mean anything to anyone?'

Norm piped up. 'Possibly. I work for an undertaker, and we buried Bessie Armstrong a few weeks ago,' he claimed.

'She wants you to know she is now free from pain and in a happy place,' enlightened Madame Holz.

The medium recommenced the séance. The two Dutch ladies were enthralled.

'This is a magnificent sessie,' whispered Lotte Bakker, unaware of the English name for séance.

'We would still like to make contact with Lawrence Boyd. If you can hear us Lawrence, we have someone in our circle who would like to express her love toward you.' Madame Holz' head twitched once more, with a stare.

'I am getting the name Roy, Royston?' Mary suddenly broke the circle.

'Oh, my goodness, that could be my ex-husband, he left me twenty years ago, is he dead?' Mary asked alarmingly.

The circle reconvened, holding hands, 'Yes, he has moved on to another world,' confirmed the Medium. 'He wanted you to know that he fathered a son, his name is also

Royston.' At that point, Mary broke the circle again and requested a double-scotch.

Shortly afterwards, the medium resumed with a similar opening prayer. She called for Lawrence Boyd once more. Annie noticed a familiar smell; like the smell she detected the night of storm Edna: a strong mildew, fusty smell of damp. Suddenly the light went out on the orange candle. Madame Holz looked uneasy.

'I am getting the letters GD, GD again, TD; these spirits seem anxious, they appear angry.'

'Stop, stop!' shouted Annie as she broke the circle. 'That could be the Devons boys,' she claimed. 'They have all died here at Ye Olde Elm Tree in recent weeks, we must not let them in.'

Annie suggested another break for refreshments. Madame Holz wore a concerned expression; she had read about the deaths, and remembered the name Devons that Annie spoke of. This was a cruel reminder for Annie.

Annie was not comfortable with the séance carrying on, but Monica was still hoping to hear from her late husband Lawrence and begged her to let the event continue. The séance resumed. Sem and Luuk had left the snug to witness the quiz-night; the séance, despite it being full of incidents, was not really their scene. Their partners, however, were captivated. Madame Holz re-lit the orange candle. She started by welcoming good spirits to join their circle, ancestors and loved ones from the astral world. She revisited the procedure, by calling to Lawrence Boyd to make himself known, which met a delayed silence. She made several more calls to try and entice Lawrence to the forum. To break the deathly silence.

Annie produced the list of names that Detective Sergeant Roach had handed her, possible surnames from the Theo grave, in the pub grounds. She handed the list to Madame Holz, and explained,

'You could try a few of these names,' whispered Annie. Madame Holz nodded and started to read the names.

'Is there anyone near the circle with the name, Theo Simkins?' Silence. 'Is there anyone in the room with the name, Theo Hawkins?' Silence again. Madame Holz looked at the long list of names and thought this was probably not going to work, but she continued. 'Is there anyone present by the name Theo Dawkins?' The curtains on each of the two snug windows flew into the room. There was a deafening crash. Annie had a sideboard full of crockery that had crashed to the floor. The circle was broken. Everyone stood up and left the table.

Norman and Bryan picked the sideboard up off the floor. The glass doors had smashed, broken crockery everywhere. Annie looked at the mess and said to herself, well at least we know his name now. Then Monica gave out a scream. Madame Holz was still sat at the table with her head slumped down on it. The assembly moved over to where she had collapsed.

'Is she in a trance?' asked Monica.

'She looks unconscious to me,' replied Mary.

Annie telephoned for the emergency services.

CHAPTER 27 – EMILIO

Mary and Bryan followed the ambulance to the hospital, albeit ten minutes behind the emergency vehicle. Madame Holz had regained consciousness in the ambulance. She did not believe it was necessary to be admitted to the hospital, however the paramedics managed to persuade her that it was in her best interest to let the medical experts examine her at least. On arrival, Mary and Bryan asked if they could see Madame Holz. It was several minutes before a hospital administrator managed to link their request with the admission of Gwendolyn Holz. The medium was sat in a chair in a waiting room; she was soon to be seen by a consultant.

'How are you Madame Holz, you gave us all a bit of a fright,' asked Mary.

'I am fine, thank you,' came the reply, 'There are some extremely angry, enraged and desperate spirits attached to Ye Olde Elm Tree. There were multiple spirits trying to enter our circle behind the spirit of Theo Dawkins. I could not cope with them all rushing at me at once. I have never experienced anything like it before, and I never want to again.'

Mary sat beside the medium and held her hand. At that moment, a nurse appeared and invited Ms Holz in to see the consultant.

Next morning, Mary arrived at Ye Olde Elm Tree. She had a copy of the Star News with her. She was hurrying, she was having an adrenaline rush. She dashed into the kitchen to find Annie. Mary provided Annie with the comprehensive detail of their discussion with Madame Holz at the hospital that night.

'What do you think it means Annie?' blurted Mary. 'She talked of angry, enraged and desperate spirits. She said there were many spirits trying to enter our circle behind that Theo chap, that caused all the damage. Madame Holz said she was overwhelmed, said she couldn't cope with all of them, at the same time.' Annie smiled at Mary.

'It was probably the Devons. They did try to break into the circle earlier in the evening, didn't they?' replied Annie.

'Oh, I almost forgot,' said Mary, 'The pub is front page news again. There was a damning report of Catheryn Devons being 'pushed' down the stairs.'

Annie sat at her kitchen table and read the report. What should she do she thought? Perhaps it is time to try and sell the old place.

Annie let Chester into the garden; the wind was becoming quite strong. There would be no excavation that day as the severe storm **Emilio** was expected.

Charles Braithwaite rang Annie from his home; he had a copy of the Star News in front of him. The headlines read 'DEVONS FAMILY MEMBER PUSHED DOWN A FLIGHT OF STAIRS AT YE OLDE ELM TREE.'

'What happened this time Annie?' asked Charles, 'Who pushed her?' Annie bit her lip in frustration.

'No one pushed her Charles, she was blind drunk, got up in the middle of the night, couldn't find her way back to her room, even tried my bedroom door, but it was locked. In the dark she must have fallen down the stairs, a freak accident. In hindsight I wish I had not let her stay the night. She used a false name when she booked the room, which tricked me,' came her reply.

'Well thank you for your side of the story Annie, I can stress to my board of directors it was a freak accident, unless we use the possibility of a poltergeist pushing her down the stairs,' suggested Charles. This proposition made Annie cross. After yesterday evenings' mayhem, she needed to play down spiritual antagonism.

'Charles, that would be ridiculous to assume that. I have lived at this old inn for ten years; I have never seen a ghost.' Annie bit her lip once more. Charles put the telephone down and realised he was not convinced. Charles entered his home office and sat down to compile an email for his directors. He had decided not to try and drive anywhere that day with the threat of another severe storm. Charles decided to support Annie's version of an accident but include the scenario of a possible poltergeist. Let us see what the board think best, Charles thought.

It was lunchtime and the rain had started driving down in the wind; storm Emilio was fast approaching. Mollie arrived at Ye Olde Elm Tree to work on the bar.

'That was exciting last night Annie,' exclaimed Mollie. 'That old sideboard crashing to the ground, the quiz-night stopped dead, everybody in the bar must have thought, what the hell was that?' Annie shook her head.

'I should not have agreed to host a séance, that was a stupid thing to do,' responded Annie.

'Which name was it again that caused the bedlam?' asked Mollie. Annie was almost too nervous to say his name in case something horrible happened.

'It was when the name of Theo Dawkins was called out,' said Annie quietly. Suddenly the air around them went icy cold. Mollie could see her breath in front of her. Annie and Mollie looked at each other quite petrified.

Annie watched the storm approaching from the pub window. The wind is getting stronger she thought; gale force gusts were pounding the nearby trees. That afternoon, Annie put in a call to business property agents Ridley and Barker. She spoke to an Ian Tomlinson and asked him for an evaluation on her public house leasehold. Mr Tomlinson asked Annie which pub was she hoping to sell.

'It's called Ye Olde Elm Tree, on Beacon Hill,' answered Annie. Before she could explain to the agent the pub's location, Ian Tomlinson interrupted,

'I know the pub well Mrs Baines, I have called in for a pint a couple of times recently. It's a very famous pub at the moment, many people are talking about it, a murder, a guy falling out of a window to his death, a darts captain with a dart in his eye. Wow, so you are looking to put Ye Olde Elm Tree on the market. I would be delighted to help you.'

Ian checked his diary. 'How about first thing Monday morning? Say 9 am,' he suggested. Annie agreed, although she hoped it would not interfere with her Monday morning cellar duties.

Detective Chief Superintendent Raj Thackeray walked past the desk of Detective Inspector Rita Judd,

'Rita, can I have a word in my office,' asked the Superintendent. DI Judd followed him into his office.

'Take a seat,' he said formally. 'As you know from several conversations recently, this department is under pressure to come up with some answers. Missing men, multiple tragic accidents, a murder and all at the same location, Ye Olde Elm Tree. My opinion has not changed; so much revolves around the licensee Annie Baines, yet we don't seem to be able to incriminate her in any way,' said Raj Thackeray who spoke in an authoritative manner.

'Yes sir, it is very frustrating, I agree sir,' replied the Inspector. The Superintendent continued,

"I have been offered a Detective Inspector from the Greater Manchester Police Department. His CV is impressive, his name is Graeme Dankworth, I rather hope he can cast a fresh eye on everything and find something that perhaps we have overlooked. He will join us Monday morning.' DI Judd looked rather contemplative.

'How will this work, sir?' she asked the Superintendent, 'Will he be working for me?' Raj Thackeray reflected on what he was to say next,

'No Rita, he will work alongside you, for one week, treat it like a handover. Introduce him to everyone at the pub, the Devons family, including the couple Richard and Catheryn, the dart player with the eye injury, the reporter attacked by birds, everyone that has been involved in some form. I will talk to Ye Olde Elm Tree, it makes sense for DI Dankworth to set up base there, and keep a close eye on the landlady, Mrs Baines.'

'What will happen after a week sir, that is not very long, considering everything involved?' asked the Inspector.

'I have arranged for a swop. It's a temporary swop, but you will be loaned out to Greater Manchester Police Department. You will head to Detective Chief Superintendent Pointon.' DI Judd looked stunned, there was a long pause,

'Where will I stay sir?' asked the Inspector.

'Ah, don't worry about that for now Rita, GMPD will find you a nice bed and breakfast, I'm sure. You need to get your head around your next assignment, and enjoy the experience, in the city. Try and get a little leisure time to yourself over the weekend.' Raj Thackeray was pleased with the way he conducted the discussion. DI Judd acknowledged the discussion had reached a close; she stood up and left his office.

Annie answered the pub's telephone; it was DCS Raj Thackeray on the line. Annie froze at first, the Superintendent had a way about him that made her nervous.

'Mrs Baines would you have a room available for the next two, possibly three or four weeks?' asked the Superintendent, 'We have a Detective Inspector Graeme Dankworth joining the team, from Greater Manchester Police Department, he is due to arrive on Monday.'

'Just a minute sir, let me check the diary,' responded Annie. Coincidentally there was only one room available for the next three weeks, the room on the top floor with the two single beds, the Toby Devons' room. 'Yes, I have one room I can offer,' Annie gave the Superintendent the price.

'It would be rather nice to have a policeman staying at Ye Olde Elm Tree, to keep us all safe,' said Annie. She hung up the phone, pondered for a moment, and wondered if this new detective believed in the supernatural.

6 pm, Annie unlocked the front door to see Monica outside waiting for the pub to open. Monica was huddled outside the porch. The strong wind had blown her umbrella inside out.

'You are keen tonight Monica,' said Annie.

'Well I wanted to discuss last night with you Annie, before the pub got too busy.' Annie poured Monica a half pint of stout, instead of her usual gin and tonic.

'That was crazy what happened last night Annie.' claimed Monica, 'Have you heard from the hospital? Any news on the medium?'

'Yes, I have. Apparently, she regained consciousness in the ambulance. Mary phoned me this afternoon; she is fine and has been discharged,' answered Annie. 'Apparently, she was overwhelmed by too many spirits trying to enter the circle through her, all at the same time. I blamed the Devons, all three of them tried to enter the circle together earlier in the evening, which is why I had to stop it.'

'It was a shame with so many spirits attached to this old pub, we never heard from my dear Lawrence, he must have moved on.' said Monica solemnly

'Yes, that was a shame,' replied Annie, 'I would have loved to have heard from your Lawrence too. Bert and I had a lot of time for Lawrence, he was a hard worker and a good friend.' Annie never mentioned the musty, damp smell, witnessed during the séance; it crossed Annie's mind; that it might have been a spirit that had drowned, in a fish pond!

Farmer Forde arrived next at the pub. 'The rain is chucking it down outside now,' he said in frustration. 'This is the third time in less than two months, I have had to shelter my girls from severe storms.'

'You spoil those cows Geoff,' came Annie's reply.

The Dutch couples returned for a few final drinks in Ye Olde Elm Tree after a day touring the local area in storm Emilio. They looked rather windswept. Lotte and Liv were still quite excited about the séance. Liv asked,

'The dead man that pulled over the china cabinet last night, is he from the historic graves or was he killed here recently?' Annie smiled, such naivety, she thought. She went to say his name, and suddenly had stop herself.

'He is buried in the first grave, the one in the bottom corner of the garden,' implied Annie.

'We have a photograph of that headstone,' Lotte stated. 'We can tell the story to our friends, when we get home, in the Netherlands. They will not believe what happened.' Their partners, Sem and Luuk, found it all very amusing.

Norman Prince popped in for pint, despite the weather. He also was hoping for an update on yesterday evening's séance. He thanked Annie for a most entertaining evening, and for introducing so many beings from the spirit world. Annie shook her head in denial.

Annie had closed the pub just after 9.30 pm as storm Emilio was reaching a peak. The Dutch couples were happy to sit in a dimly lit pub to finish off the evening, in fact they considered it quite romantic. It was a restless night for

Annie. At times like this; she worried about the storm causing damage to the property. Under her leasehold contract with the pub company, she was responsible for the maintenance of the building. Another reason to possibly sell up soon.

Next morning, the storm seemed to have passed. The weather was dull, a drizzle, a few wild gusts of wind. Chester was keen for his morning venture into the garden. He went straight to the grave of Theo Dawkins and sat down. Annie put on her boots and followed him. The ground was extremely wet, like a quagmire in places. Annie reached the grave and could not believe what she was looking at. The Theo grave had been filled in with mud, so had the grave next to it, where the archaeologists had removed the woman and child skeletons. Two new headstones had been exposed by the mud slide. One grave had a stone marker only, an unnamed grave. The other grave had a slate headstone which had collapsed onto a kerbed grave. Annie looked at the two graves and reflected on the difference in the graves; the wealth of one, compared to the other. Annie looked sorrowful and worried.

CHAPTER 28 – THE NEW DETECTIVE

Annie telephoned Detective Inspector Judd to tell her about the discovery of two new gravestones. Annie had to leave her a telephone answer message.

'Hello Inspector, this is Annie Baines at Ye Olde Elm Tree. The storm Emilio yesterday has caused a landslide in the pub garden. Unfortunately, most of the mud has engulfed the new Theo and mother and son graves, however, there are two new gravestones exposed. Hope you have a good weekend.'

DI Judd later heard the message but decided to ignore it until the Monday morning. After all, Detective Chief Superintendent Thackeray instructed her to try and enjoy some leisure time over the weekend, before she is to be loaned out to the Greater Manchester Police Department, the following week.

That morning, over breakfast, the two Dutch ladies were still talking about the séance.

'Mrs Baines, can we have another session with that Madame the medium?'" asked Lottie. Annie smiled,

'I am not sure she would want to return to Ye Olde Elm Tree, there are too many spirits living here,' claimed Annie.

'Let us wish for a ghost to join us for breakfast,' suggested Liv.

Instantly, a photograph on the wall fell to the ground. It was an old photograph of the public house, when it was called the King's Arms. Lottie and Liv looked at each other horrified. Sem and Luuk looked troubled. Annie walked over to the picture and picked it up off the floor. The glass had broken.

Detective Inspector Dankworth; forty-two, six feet, muscular build, visits the local gym regularly, divorced for five years, married to the force now, two teenage sons. He had promised to take the boys for a canal cruise on the Sunday morning, followed by tickets for a Premiership football game in the afternoon. Thus, Graeme was having to pack his suitcase for the Monday morning, on the Saturday. It was the first time his suitcase had been used in six years. His last holiday was with the family to Florida. He was quite excited about the new challenge ahead.

Annie asked Mollie and Jimmy to cover the bar on the lunchtime that day. Annie had to visit the local town to replace the crockery that was broken in the séance. Annie still regretted hosting the event. Before she had left, she was cornered by Brigit and Mary. Brigit wanted to hear all about the séance. She was so disappointed; she could have joined in the séance after all as her blind date never showed up. Mary suggested exorcism, next.

 Annie shook her head, 'Oh no, certainly not,' said Annie.

Monday morning soon came around for DI Judd. She met the 8.45 am train from Manchester at the local station. She recognised Detective Inspector Dankworth straight away, in his full uniform. They drove straight to the local police station, where DCS Raj Thackeray welcomed Graeme Dankworth to the department and introduced him to the team. DI Judd made two telephone calls, one to Annie at Ye Olde Elm Tree to notify her of DI Dankworth's arrival and they would soon be paying her a visit, the other to Dr Cynthia Bell to inform her of the two new grave findings, following storm Emilio.

Annie Baines decided to postpone her cellar work that morning, to the following day. At 9 am, Ian Tomlinson, from property agents Ridley and Barker, arrived at Ye Olde Elm Tree. He stood outside for a while admiring the building. Annie gave him a guided tour of the public house, whilst Mary looked after the Dutch party with their breakfasts. Ian commented on the restricted small kitchen. Annie explained that neither her, nor her late husband were interested in the catering side of the business, we were quite happy with mostly wet sales. She also explained the seasonality of the trade. Annie proceeded to show Mr Tomlinson the private quarters, and the bed and breakfast accommodation. When they entered the Toby Devons bedroom, she felt a quiver. Her throat went dry when Ian Tomlinson asked,

'Is this the window where one of your guests fell from?' Annie did not answer him, she just acknowledged his question.

Annie took the agent into the large pub garden. She explained about the historic digs that have taken place, and she pointed out the two new graves exposed by the recent storm. Ian Tomlinson was astonished at the potential, the tourist opportunity the pub grounds had to offer. For Ian to provide a valuation, he explained to Annie, how her pub was an extraordinary unique property and unusual business to market; his estimated evaluation was five-fold what Bert and Annie had paid for it, ten years earlier. Annie was astonished.

Before Ian Tomlinson had left Ye Olde Elm Tree, DI Judd and DI Dankworth had arrived. Annie explained to Mr Tomlinson that there was a new detective from Manchester who was booked into one of the rooms for a few weeks. Ian Tomlinson was suitably impressed. DI Judd introduced DI Dankworth to Annie.

'Who was that?' Di Judd asked Annie, pointing at Ian Tomlinson. 'He seemed very business-like.'

'He works for Ridley and Barker, Business Property Agents,' replied Annie. Detective Inspector Dankworth jumped in,

'Are you selling up and moving on?' he snapped.

'No,' responded Annie, 'I just wanted to have the business valued.' At this point, DI Judd jumped in,

'How did you perceive the valuation Mrs Baines?' she asked. Annie paused to think through her answer,

'On a par with my expectations really,' claimed Annie.

DI Judd asked Annie if she could show DI Dankworth around Ye Olde Elm Tree, both inside and outside. Annie agreed to just let them loose. The two police officers started with the car park, where allegedly, for the local constabulary, it all began.

Charles Braithwaite made a lunchtime visit to Teddy Valentine, landlord at the Burton Arms. Teddy took the opportunity to bleat at Charles, that the landlady at Ye Olde Elm Tree had hosted a séance.

'It all went terribly wrong with a poltergeist smashing a china cabinet' claimed Teddy.

How interesting thought Charles. After the visit, Charles returned to his car and telephoned his director Douglas Winterbottom with the news.

'Good story Charles, dear chap, well done old boy,' acknowledged Douglas. 'I think I will feed that story to my good friend, the editor at Star News.'

Doctors Cynthia Bell and David Donnelly arrived at Ye Olde Elm Tree early afternoon. They were both fascinated by the new discovery of the two gravestones with such a difference in status. Their priority was to try and lift the headstone on the kerbed grave. Contractor George Pullman arrived next, which was good news. They carefully lifted the headstone to find most of it intact, perhaps protected from the elements by it resting on the grave. Eleanor Thornley. Loved wife to Aldrich. Mother to (was not readable). Died seventeenth day of May 1908. Time for Dr Bell to contact local historian Claudette Quail.

Late that afternoon, Annie took a call from Colin Coombes, the editor of the Star News. He enquired about the séance that took place at the pub recently. Annie shuddered; how did they get to find out about this? she wondered. Colin asked if he could send a reporter to Ye Olde Elm Tree for an interview with Annie. She played the telephone interview card. Mr Coombes was insistent this time, for a reporter and photographer to descend on the pub. He also asked of the names for all those that did attend the séance. Annie gave his request some thought and replied,

'I think you should get the permission of the medium that conducted the séance before I provide you with any names Mr Coombes. Her trading name is Madame Holz.'

Nightmares at Ye Olde Elm Tree

Colin Coombes laughed down the telephone and promised to send a team to Ye Olde Elm Tree that same day. Putting the telephone down, Annie considered that quite a rude reaction.

Annie made four telephone calls. The first was to her sister Nancy, wanting to tell her of the leasehold evaluation of Ye Olde Elm Tree. The second was to Ian Tomlinson instructing him to represent the sale of Ye Olde Elm Tree. Ian Tomlinson was delighted. Her third call was to Charles Braithwaite, to notify him of her intention to sell the lease.

'But why Annie?' asked Charles, 'You have so much going for you at the moment.'

'It is all too much for me Charles,' came her reply, 'If Bert was still alive, maybe it would be different, it's just too much for me now, with all the recent shenanigans and trying to run the old place, on my own.'

Charles asked, 'Annie, what was the estimated value of Ye Olde Elm Tree?' He was impressed at how high the valuation was. He put the telephone down and straight away wrote an email to notify his board of directors.

The fourth telephone call was to an American family stopping at Ye Olde Elm Tree the following weekend. It was a mobile number, as the Gonzalez family should already be in the UK touring. She had the names, Benjamin and Abigail, Lucas and Mia, Pops and Nanny. Annie assumed the latter were grandparents. She got through to Mrs Gonzalez, who confirmed they were already in the country. Annie decided to work out sleeping arrangements for when they would arrive on the Friday.

That evening, the bar was busy once more. DI Dankworth was in casual clothing drinking lager and lemonade shandies. He spoke to many of the locals about Ye Olde Elm Tree, the possible hauntings, the excavations, missing persons, the séance, the murder, the historic findings, and more. His appetite for information on the old inn was intense. Annie asked Mollie if she could cover the bar for the rest of the evening; Annie was fed up with Inspector Dankworth already. She retired to her lounge upstairs.

That evening, DI Dankworth was early to bed. The travel, trying to take in all the facts about Ye Olde Elm Tree, he was shattered. I will sleep well tonight he thought. It was approximately 3 am in the morning, the detective woke with a start, his body jerked. It was as if someone had sat on the bottom of his bed. Unfortunately for the Inspector, he was now quite awake. He focused on the bedroom window, reflecting on what he was told regarding Toby Devons. He rose and went to the window. It was an overcast night, no moon to light up the garden below. He suddenly focussed on the new Thornley grave. There seemed to be four or five bodies kneeling, around the grave, they were quite immobile. Just the occasional movement. This is mad, he thought. He would discuss it with Mrs Baines in the morning.

At breakfast, DI Dankworth explained to Annie what he thought he saw that night. Annie dismissed it, as if it probably never happened. The Inspector asked,

'Should there be a repeat of whatever I saw in the garden last night, tonight; would you mind Mrs Baines, if I could enter your garden, to check it out?'

'Not at all,' responded Annie, 'More coffee Officer?' changing the subject.

DI Judd had nonchalantly planned several busy days for DI Dankworth. They would try and fit in interviews with the Devons' parents, a journey to the West Midlands to meet Richard and Catheryn Devons, reporter Nick Fitzsimons, Julian Jameson, who found Garrett Devons, and the Burton Arms darts captain Ruben Hagen, for starters.

Director Douglas Winterbottom telephoned his nephew Fraser to inform him that Ye Olde Elm Tree was on the market and gave him the value. Fraser and his wife Melanie used to run a public house in a nearby town. They sold up and moved to the coast to run a bed and breakfast, but Fraser was not enjoying it; he much preferred the pub life. Coincidentally, Fraser and his uncle Douglas were only discussing the other day, Ye Olde Elm Tree and everything that had taken place there in recent weeks.

'It is haunted, lots of ghosts mind Fraser,' joked his uncle. They both laughed down the telephone. Fraser decided to contact Ridley and Barker for more details; he spoke to Ian Tomlinson.

'We have only just received instructions on the property however we aim to have the details on our website for this evening,' claimed the Agent. 'Would you like to arrange a viewing?' he asked.

'Yes please,' replied Fraser, 'Any afternoon this week would be excellent.'

Historian Claudette Quail telephoned Dr Cynthia Bell; she had made significant progress with the two enquiries that the anthropologist had provided. Theo Dawkins was a Hooper by trade. Forging metal hoops for beer barrels and the like. Born 1860 died 1902. In the 1861, 1871, 1881 and 1891 censuses he lived with his parents, he was one of six siblings, three elder brothers and two elder sisters. In the 1901 census he lived alone with his mother at a new address. Marriageable status, bachelor.

On Eleanor Thornley there was much more information available, including two front page news articles from 1908. Eleanor and her husband Aldrich lived at Heppleton Manor, with their two sons. Aldrich in the 1901 census was listed as a Gun Journeyman, Trader to Asia. On the 17th March 1908 Aldrich found his wife Eleanor in their summer house with their gardener. In a rage he returned to the main house, loaded his shotgun, and killed them both, as they were wrapped in arms together. Their gardener was of an ethnic difference. It made front page news the following day.

In another report, one week later, Aldrich Thornley paid a considerable amount of money to have them buried together, to live out their sin, indefinitely.

That evening at Ye Olde Elm Tree it was card school night. The Detective Inspector sat at the bar close to the four players and watched them intensely. He was surprised at how competitive they were. On settling down for the night, he set his alarm on his mobile phone for 3 am. He was keen to explore any unusual eerie happenings in the pub garden. His alarm went off. He went to his bathroom and threw cold water over his face to wake himself up. He stared out of his bedroom window; the night was again overcast, with quite a high wind. He fixed his eyes on the Thornley grave. There they were again, four or five figures huddled around the grave. He impetuously got dressed, grabbed his mobile phone, unlocked his bedroom door, and proceeded down two flights of stairs to the kitchen, and back door. He fumbled with the keys for the door for a moment, but was soon in the garden, racing toward the Thornley grave, trying to pick out the figures with the torch on his mobile phone. The figures, like silhouettes, seemed to stare at him, but they were faceless. He was within ten yards of the grave, when the figures seemed to disperse in many different directions. They scattered, then disappeared. Where did they go, asked the Inspector? Where are they now? They have totally vanished! The detective shone his torch around in all directions; the night was suddenly motionless. DI Dankworth did not believe in the paranormal, perhaps this was to be his first celestial experience.

CHAPTER 29 – GOODBYE DETECTIVE

The next morning, Detective Inspector Dankworth confronted Annie at the breakfast table. He explained what he had seen that night, how he rushed down to the garden and as he approached these dark figures, they dispersed in different directions, completely vanishing. Annie tried to stare at the Inspector inquisitively, trying to wear an expression that he must have imagined it.

'Sorry Inspector but I have lived here ten years or more. I have never seen any figures in the garden; having said that, I tend not to go into the garden in the middle of the night,' responded Annie.

The Inspector detected a hint of sarcasm, antagonism in her reply. Can I trust her? he thought.

That morning, Madame Holz received a telephone call from Star News reporter, Godfrey Wallace. He explained how his newspaper was keen to run a story on her séance at Ye Olde Elm Tree. The medium treated the request as free publicity and agreed to meet, that day.

Dr Bell and Dr Donnelly met contractor George Pullman at Ye Olde Elm Tree at 10 am, as arranged. They decided to carry on with the excavations and start a new dig next to the unmarked grave.

Annie received a telephone call from Ian Tomlinson at Ridley and Barker. He was keen to arrange a first viewing of Ye Olde Elm Tree. Annie thought that was quick work.

That morning, DI Judd and DI Dankworth drove to the home of Richard and Catheryn Devons. They lived in an apartment block. There was a very vicious looking dog to walk past to reach their apartment, number fifteen. Both Richard and Catheryn were adamant that landlady Annie Baines had pushed Catheryn down the stairs.

'She had time to open her bedroom door, push me down the stairs, re-enter her bedroom and lock the door, before the Polish visitor ever came to the scene,' implied Catheryn passionately. She was still in a neck brace, arm in a sling, shoulder strapped, recovering from her ordeal. DI Dankworth was slowly suspecting Annie Baines more and more, for the accidents and the murder at Ye Olde Elm Tree.

By midday, contractor George had uncovered a new gravestone. It was next to the unmarked grave. A cast stone memorial block headstone. After a good clean, the headstone read, Cedric William Huxley, beloved husband to Gladys. No date. This is another name for historian Claudette Quail, thought Dr Bell.

That evening, Ye Olde Elm Tree darts team were hosts to the Cat and the Fiddle, a nearby town centre pub. The competition turned out to be quite a young team. DI Dankworth sat at the bar, questioning their ages. Annie asked them all for identification. Two of the team were unable to produce ID so Annie had to refuse to sell them alcohol. The Inspector watched this carefully all evening, much to Annie's annoyance. At least her darts team won, five-two.

That night, DI Dankworth was woken by someone tapping on his bedroom door. It was a faint, tap, tap, tap. It was persistent. He jumped out of bed, made himself presentable and reached for his mobile phone. Unlatching the door, he shone his torch into the corridor, there was no one there. He proceeded down the stairs to Annie's room.

'Mrs Baines,' he called out. Eventually Annie unlatched her bedroom door and squared up to the officer. They had a confrontation about the tapping on the detective's bedroom door! The Inspector uncharacteristically said,

'I suppose you would like to push me down the stairs next, Mrs Baines.' Annie looked daggers at the detective.

She wished him 'Goodnight,' and slammed her bedroom door shut. DI Dankworth was infuriated.

The following morning, Mary arrived with a copy of the Star News.

'Front page news again Annie,' she joked, 'You will soon be on reality TV at this rate!'

The headlines read 'SÉANCE AT YE OLDE ELM TREE BRINGS THE SUPERNATURAL TO LIFE.' There was an entire exposition of the Madame Holz séance at Ye Olde Elm tree. There was a generous photograph of Madame Holz, minutiae of the first visitation, from the initials BA, elderly Bessie Armstrong, a spirit passed to the other side quite peacefully. Next was the name Roy, Royston, which transpired to be a former husband of one of the participants in the circle. The spirit made it known that he had fathered a child with another woman. The medium received the initials GD, GD, TD, and how the landlady panicked and stopped the séance. One GD killed by a freak accident, another GD murdered by a garden fork, and TD who committed suicide, throwing himself from a top floor window, all at Ye Olde Elm Tree. Then the feature magnified the crescendo with the naming of the Theo Dawkins spirit, buried in the inn grounds for approximately one hundred years. The spirit demolished a china cabinet in the pub's small bar, where the séance was being held. Annie read this and slumped into her kitchen chair. There is no point trying to deny a transcendent presence after this damning report, she thought.

Mary agreed; she was annoyed that Madame Holz had reported Royston and the child, born to another woman.

DI Judd took DI Dankworth to meet up with reporter Nick Fitzsimons. This interview unnerved the Inspector after his experience the previous evening. The reporter became quite hysterical telling the officers about his encounter with flocks of birds that had attacked him, and disappearing shadows. DI Dankworth could relate to the shadows, which disturbed him. The reporter broke down afterwards and sobbed. Later back in the police car, Di Judd observed,

'He really hasn't recovered from that frightening experience he had with those birds. Very strange.' Di Dankworth frowned at his fellow officer.

Annie was quite excited by a viewing of Ye Olde Elm Tree. Fraser and Melanie Winterbottom stood outside the front of the pub for what seemed ages. That is an encouraging sign, thought Annie. She showed them around the licenced premises, accommodation, and grounds. Melanie was keen to extend the kitchen facilities, increase the food trade. Fraser was enthralled by the garden, the local history uncovered and the ongoing potential. Fraser had a lengthy conversation with archaeologist Dr Donnelly; he was sold on Ye Olde Elm Tree after that.

Later that day, Annie made two visits. One was to the local veterinary practice with Chester. Her soulmate was off his food and was noticeably more lethargic than usual. The vet suggested to retain Chester overnight and run a few tests on him. Annie reluctantly agreed.

The second was to the local vicarage. She had set up a meeting with Reverend Christopher Sallow to discuss the possibility of exorcism. Rev Sallow made a pot of tea whilst Annie gave the vicar the background on Ye Olde Elm Tree. The number of potential spirits in the old inn was rife. Annie's once gardener, her late husband, his sister, the three Devons' relatives. She explained to the pastor how they had all died; the three salesmen, she detailed that atrocious ordeal; the Catheryn Devons' accident, the missing photographer, the reporter and the bird attack; the historic graves that had been uncovered. Annie went on to explain the outcome of the séance.

Rev Sallow looked at Annie with a fearful expression. He explained to Annie that Anglican priests may not perform an exorcism without the permission from the Diocesan bishop. He did offer to at least speak to his bishop when they next meet and he would have to raise each of the incidents that he had logged, that had taken place at Ye Olde Elm Tree. He went on to explain that an exorcism is quite rare, these days. It has been known that the bishop would often be in attendance to conduct a blessing. On earlier occasions the bishop had carefully selected a team of specialists to approve an exorcism on a person, such as a psychiatrist, a physician and in some special cases, representation from local government mental health. There was one experience, he knew of, in Wiltshire where even the police were called upon. When it comes to property exorcism the bishop may call upon expertise of a different nature, for example a spiritualist. In Hampshire he once met a Diocese exorcist. Sometimes the bishop may request prowess from different religions, depending on the circumstances. Annie thanked him for his time and guidance. She told him how she had recently engaged the sale of the pub business so it was probably best she should sleep on the whole idea of exorcism, for now.

That afternoon, DI Dankworth approached the office of Detective Chief Superintendent Thackeray. He had an exciting proposal he wanted to run past the Superintendent. Entering his office, he told the senior officer how he had been studying a thermal imaging drone that the Armed Forces use to locate unexploded bombs, depth charges and land mines. The MK 1V DRTI X9 had a range of up to twenty-five to thirty metre thermal imaging underground, depending on rock construction.

'It would be ideal to trace the alleged vehicle below Ye Olde Elm Tree car park, which consists of shingle on top of soil,' claimed the Inspector. Raj Thackeray looked interested,

'Can you get one Graeme?' asked the Superintendent.

'I have spoken to a good contact of mine at the Greater Manchester barracks, and yes we can hire the model per day,' replied DI Dankworth.

'Hire, how much?' enquired Raj Thackeray.

'To hire, not a lot, one thousand pounds per day. There are add on costs though; an army officer to fly it and a transporter vehicle. Three Grand altogether.' The DCS grimaced.

'That's a budget we just do not have Graeme,' replied the Superintendent.

'I realise it is hell of a lot of money sir, but consider this, if there is a vehicle under the car park, this drone will find it. If it does not find a car then the suspicion can be placed back on Annie Baines, for wasting police time and money, with outright lies. What else has she lied about? Where are the three salesmen? Or better still, where are their bodies? It will prove it, one way or the other. It would help us to get the salesmen's barrister off our backs. We may even be able to charge Annie Baines with perverting the course of justice,' responded DI Dankworth. DCS Thackeray shook his head and roared,

'Let's do it Graeme.'

That evening it was quiz night, with Alfie Richardson. DI Dankworth was not in a quiz team, although he did have a question and answer sheet to fill in. The highest scoring team scored twenty correct answers. Graeme Dankworth was feeling rather pleased with himself, he also scored twenty, on his own. He also took great delight in telling Annie that his department are to hire a drone from the Armed Forces with a thermal imagine camera, with a range underground of up to thirty metres.

'We will find that missing car for you Mrs Baines, with all those dead bodies in it. The drone will arrive tomorrow afternoon,' the Inspector said with contempt. Annie felt palpitations with this news. To revisit that awful scene would be devastating for Annie.

During the night, there was a scraping and scratching on DI Dankworth's bedroom door. He did unlatch his door and shine his mobile phone torch up and down the corridor. With nothing to be seen, he decided not to confront Annie Baines this time, and returned to his bed.

Next morning Annie received two telephone calls. The first one caused her anxiety. Chester had been tested and was ready to go home; sadly, the X-rays had identified a few tumours. Her second call, a few minutes later, changed the mood completely. Fraser Winterbottom had made her an offer for the pub lease, five thousand pounds under the asking price. That was still a good offer, thought Annie.

Later that morning the Gonzalez family arrived. There was much confusion over the sleeping arrangements; it took Annie over twenty minutes to establish who would be staying in which room. The conclusion was Mr & Mrs Gonzalez would go on the top floor next to DI Dankworth's room. Mia would share with Nanny and Lucas with Pops on the first floor. The Gonzalez children were fascinated with the archaeological excavations taking place, especially as contractor George had dug down to another coffin lid that morning of Cedric William Huxley.

That afternoon the Armed Forces vehicle arrived. DI Dankworth and DS Roach were at Ye Olde Elm Tree to greet it. They set up the drone after lunchtime closing. DI Dankworth did not want any vehicles in the pub car park, that could possibly interfere with the images. Annie was forced to move her Morris Minor onto the road, into the nearby layby. It took only minutes for the drone to pick up the image of the car. It was in the centre of the car park, approximately one metre below the surface. When the army officer showed the police officers the images, DS Roach admitted to DI Dankworth,

'We didn't dig in the centre of the car park Guv, we only dug in several locations, at the far end.'

A few telephone calls were then made. DI Dankworth telephoned DCS Thackeray with the news. He in turn telephoned Donald Rutherford SC, the barrister representing the families of the missing salesmen.

DS Roach telephoned contractor George Pullman, who had left site in a hurry that afternoon, covering the new grave over with only a tarpaulin sheet, which was all he had with him. The DS announced that they were planning to excavate the car park once again, over the weekend. They had identified where the missing car was, they would need heavy lifting gear as well this time. George Pullman was elated.

DS Roach then telephoned DI Judd with the news. The Inspector had been in the office all day to tie up loose ends before she would be loaned out to Greater Manchester Police Department. DI Judd had already heard the news from DCS Thackeray, who had jubilantly passed her desk, five minutes earlier. The Inspector felt dispirited, depressed.

DI Dankworth had great pleasure in notifying Annie of the discovery. Annie could not watch the army drone, for fear of what it might find. Afterwards, she became apprehensive, fearful, and bemused.

Nobody knew why DI Judd did not go straight home that evening; instead she drove to Ye Olde Elm Tree. She had passed DI Dankworth's police vehicle and Mrs Baines' Morris Minor in the layby. She soon realised they were probably parked there because of the drone survey. DI Judd parked in the empty pub car park and made her way into the back garden. She walked along the line of unearthed graves. She stopped at the new grave of Cedric William Huxley, read the inscription; no date she pondered. She also wondered why George had used tarpaulin to cover the dug grave, especially after the Rachel Hooper sleepwalking incident. Deep down, DI Judd blamed this quintessential old English inn for everything that had happened to her and why she was being loaned out to Greater Manchester Police Department.

She had reached the point of blaming the supernatural, the telekinesis for her failures. She grew angry, full of hatred, her fists clenched; it was almost as if she had become possessed. She shouted continuous abuse to the spirits. She swore at the spirits. She shouted harmful, injurious assertions; she told them all to go to hell. She had become an abomination. It was then, someone, something, pushed the Inspector hard in her back. She fell onto the tarpaulin. It gave way on one side with her weight, and she fell into the dugout grave. She struck her head; she was concussed, confused. It was not the fall that killed the detective, it was the large granite rock that was dropped on the back of her head.

CHAPTER 30 – THE UNEARTHING

It was early Friday evening, Detective Inspector Dankworth, had changed from his uniform into casual clothes. He was feeling rather pleased with his week's work. Persuading Detective Chief Superintendent Thackeray to invest in the thermal imaging camara and finding the location of the missing vehicle. He decided to move his car from the nearby layby; he was not comfortable with his police car parked on the open road. He exited Ye Olde Elm Tree through the front door, when he glanced at a police car in the pub car park. My car's been moved was his first thought. He walked over to the car a little bewildered. On inspection, he noticed quite bad scratches on the nearside front wing. Wait a minute, he thought, that's Rita's vehicle. She must be in the grounds, as he had just walked through the pub bar, and she was not inside.

'Rita, Rita,' the DI called, and again, 'Rita.' He noticed the collapsed tarpaulin on the new Huxley grave, and walked over to it.

'Oh my God,' he hollered. There was DI Judd laying in the grave, not moving, a large rock laying on the back of her head. Without thinking, he jumped down into the grave. With great difficulty he managed to lift the rock out of the grave and rest it on the grass by the side.

Blowing his cheeks, he said to himself, that was bloody heavy. He looked again at the Detective Inspector; her head, splattered in blood. He took her wrist, there was no pulse. DI Dankworth heaved himself up out of the grave and ran back into Ye Olde Elm Tree. Annie was behind the bar emptying glasses from the dishwasher.

'I've got to call the emergency services. DI Judd looks to have been killed in one of your graves,' he howled at her.

The emergency services arrived in force. Paramedics ambulance, EMS ambulance, two police cars; one belonged to Detective Chief Superintendent Raj Thackeray. He had been notified of the tragedy by his front desk at the station. Detective Inspector Rita Judd was confirmed dead. The medics and the police agreed that a post-mortem would be necessary. Annie ventured into the car park, where the Superintendent questioned her about DI Judd, but she claimed to know nothing about it, as she had been all afternoon inside the pub.

The DCS instructed Annie to close her pub for the foreseeable future, at least until after the next excavation the following day, to disinter the buried vehicle in the car park. Annie informed the officer that she could not close the pub that evening. Being Friday, it was full of locals, most of which were already in the bar. The Superintendent told Annie that he would put a constable outside the pub to stop any more customers arriving. Annie reluctantly put a chalk board outside Ye Olde Elm Tree. 'Sorry. Closed this evening.'

Farmers Geoffrey Forde and Granville, Monica, Desmond People and Alice, card school Jules and Badger, several of the dart team including Charlie Hind were amongst several punters waiting for Annie to return to the bar. They were all keen to learn the latest gossip on the dead policewoman.

The next morning DI Dankworth remembered his car parked on the road in the layby. As he approached the vehicle, he noticed red paint sprayed on the car door. 'Pigs.'

He could not believe it. Who the hell would do that? he thought, Mrs Baines? The detective re-entered Ye Olde Elm Tree and raced through the bar and into the kitchen where Annie was clearing up after his breakfast.

'Where have you hidden it Mrs Baines?' wailed the Inspector.

'Hidden what?' asked Annie.

'A can of red spray paint, that has damaged my police vehicle,' was his reply.

'Have you gone mad Officer?' enquired Annie.

'I need you to open your shed up for me, so I can look for the spray can,' insisted DI Dankworth.

'Where is your search warrant?' Annie said confidently. The Inspector backed off, but he was seething.

Saturday morning, contractor George Pullman was the first to arrive at Ye Olde Elm Tree with his JCB 5CX Eco Backhoe Loader. Detective Sergeant Roach was next to arrive with Detective Constable Frank Prewitt. DI Dankworth was in his element supervising George on where to commence the dig. DC Prewitt was roadside at the front of Ye Olde Elm Tree, redirecting traffic away from the pub. The two doctors, Bell and Donnelly, were the next to arrive. George was about to start when the DAF truck with HYVA crane car recovery system arrived. Annie saw this and thought she should not really watch the next events; she had already telephoned Mollie and explained the pub was going to be closed for the day.

George went down approximately one metre when there was a clunk and the sound of breaking glass. George's Backhoe Loader had struck the back window of the

Mercedes. Normally a vehicle would be wheel clamped to be hoisted up onto the DAF truck, but on this occasion the car wheels were truly buried. This was going to be an unusual lift, thought DI Dankworth. It was decided to break the remaining windows of the car and attach hoist straps to the car roof. As the car windows were broken one by one, the stench from the rotting bodies inside the car was most unpleasant. DS Roach struggled to cope with it. At least the driver's door window was already broken, just as Annie Baines had once described. DI Dankworth telephoned DCS Thackeray with the news of two bodies inside the vehicle.

That checks out with Mrs Baines' account the Superintendent thought. They agreed once the car had been crane lifted onto the truck and taken away to the forensic yard, that they would continue to dig for the third body. Half an hour on, George's bucket jaw hooked onto a trouser belt; the two doctors were given the unpleasant task of exhuming the rest of body; the stench was most unpleasant. They both agreed dental records would be the best method to identify the three men. Annie watched all this happen from the apex window on the top floor; the very window she watched that disaster unfold one Monday evening several months earlier.

Annie made herself a cup of tea, she was distraught. She had, had enough. Time to do something about the inane situation. She telephoned Ridley and Barker Property Agents and spoke to Ian Tomlinson. She was ready to accept Mr and Mrs Winterbottom's offer for the sale of the pub's leasehold contract.

'Excellent, Mrs Baines,' Ian replied, 'I will let Fraser Winterbottom know straight away. He has instructed our company to represent the sale of their bed and breakfast business once a deal had been agreed.'

Annie put the phone down, her lip quivering; this was to be a new chapter in her life. She prayed for the forgiveness of her late husband Bert.

The Gonzalez family were planning a boat trip on the local lake that day, but there was far too much excitement going on at Ye Olde Elm Tree. The family watched the car being hauled out of the ground by the crane recovery vehicle. Lucas was not looking forward to the planned short vacation in the UK, but he was now relishing his stay at Ye Olde Elm Tree. Mia was a little young to fully understand what was taking place. They watched it from outside the pub; DC Prewitt made sure they did not get too close to the unearthing. Once the car was taken away, Mr Gonzalez insisted they went on their boat trip. It was probably fortunate for them that they missed the third body discovery and unearthing. They all trudged off to the nearby layby where their campervan was parked.

6 pm on that Saturday evening, Farmer Forde was the first to arrive. Annie met him at the front door and directed him to park his Jeep in the nearby layby. The police had cordoned off the entrance to Ye Olde Elm Tree car park. Annie had a closed notice outside the pub but was determined to let a few of her locals have a drink behind closed doors. Monica, Granville, Terry Thornley & Ray Titcombe, Eddie & Barbara, Desmond and Alice, Jules Jameson, were all let in for a drink. Vehicles were scattered on the grass verges on the main road. DI Dankworth returned to Ye Olde Elm Tree at approximately 7.30 pm. He

made it known to Annie that she should have closed the pub altogether and not let her local customers in at all. He also announced he was planning to check out of the inn the following morning, as his business was over at Ye Olde Elm Tree. Annie thought that rather peculiar.

In the middle of the night, DI Dankworth was woken with a start. There was commotion in the corridor outside his bedroom door. He opened his eyes; he could hardly see across his bedroom, as there was a mist pouring into his room from an open chimney and fireplace. The air was freezing cold. A damp, musty smell was in the air. Making himself presentable rather expeditiously, he unlatched his door to see Mr and Mrs Gonzalez in the passageway. They pointed to their bedroom. Mrs Gonzalez looked terrified; there was a freezing cold mist filling their bedroom as well, through the open chimney. DI Dankworth rushed downstairs and hollered outside Annie's bedroom door.

'Mrs Baines, you need to come upstairs straight away.'

She unlatched her bedroom door to see the Inspector and Mr and Mrs Gonzalez outside her room. Annie rushed upstairs, entered each room and opened the windows. The mist slowly started to clear. She could not help but notice that there was no mist outside the building.

'It will clear in a few minutes. We can all go back to bed,' said Annie, trying to stay calm. It was afterwards that DI Dankworth tried to analyse what had just happened; how did Mrs Baines pull off such a stunt? Witchcraft came to mind.

The next morning, DI Dankworth checked out of Ye Olde Elm Tree after breakfast. His silence over breakfast was eerie. Afterwards, Annie reflected on the strained atmosphere over breakfast, and thought she had preferred some of the heated conversations and accusations, she had previously with the detective, rather than the baleful behaviour that morning.

Annie never opened Ye Olde Elm Tree that day; the police had promised to re-level the car park on the Monday. The anthropologist and the archaeologist were also planning to return that day for potentially more excavation work. What Annie did not know was that DI Dankworth had booked into a local hotel just two miles away.

Monday morning, DI Dankworth was summoned to DCS Thackeray's office.

'So, Graeme I understand forensic are checking the dental records of the three salesmen and we should have the results by hopefully tomorrow, at the latest,' stated the Superintendent.

'That's correct sir,' replied the Inspector. 'Do you think we should bring licensee Mrs Baines in for questioning, once more?' asked DI Dankworth.

'We had to let her go last time Graeme,' answered DCS Thackeray. 'We never had enough proof for a conviction.' Di Dankworth stroked his chin,

'We could bring her in on a charge of perverting the **course of justice**,' claimed the Inspector. She had you all digging up the car park in the wrong places. Why was that, to save her own skin?' remarked DI Dankworth.

'Yes Graeme, a total waste of our time, and resource,' replied DCS Thackeray, 'Let us have one more try with her, check her story thoroughly with her previous statements. She may be unsettled by us unearthing that vehicle.'

DI Dankworth and DS Roach drove to Ye Olde Elm Tree to arrest Annie Baines, for a second time. The Gonzalez family had just checked out, having had a wonderful stay. Annie had just checked the diary for the following weekend; two rooms only booked. A Mr and Mrs King, and a Mr Gough and a Mr McSorley, sharing. She could vacate the top floor next weekend, she was relieved. The two officers cautioned Annie and led her away to the station. She was allowed three telephone calls; Mary to look in on Chester, Mollie to tell her Ye Olde Elm Tree would not be opening that day, (she blamed the upheaval in the car park) and to Reginald Spearing, her old friend and solicitor.

Reginald Spearing was unable to reach the police station until 2 pm that day. DI Dankworth suggested for Annie to sit in a draughty corridor, rather than in the interview room. Give her plenty of time to fester. She did find a few conversations of interest; she overheard detective constable Liz Brentwood call out to DI Dankworth that there were no other fingerprints or DNA on the rock that landed on Inspector Judd, other than his.

DI Dankworth started the interview with, 'It is ten minutes past two. I am here with licensee Mrs Annie Baines from Ye Olde Elm Tree Inn, Beacon Hill. She is accompanied by her legal representation, Mr Reginald Spearing. I am Detective Inspector Graeme Dankworth and I am joined by Detective Sergeant Jafari Dhowre.'

The Inspector did not ask DS Roach in on the interview as he was a common factor on the previous interview. He continued,

'Please Mrs Baines, can you tell us once more, very carefully, step by step, what you saw that evening, when the three salesmen's vehicle entered your public house car park.' Annie gave an account the best she could; it was upsetting for her.

'Mrs Baines,' chipped in the Inspector, 'Surely the far corner of the car park, is a downright lie. We all know the vehicle was recovered in the centre of the car park, as did you, Mrs Baines, on that regretful evening.' DI Dankworth raised his voice to inflict authority.

Annie swore that it all happened in the far corner. She could not explain how the car ended up in the centre; it must have moved with the bad weather.

The interview went on, with a few breaks, for a gruelling three hours. DI Dankworth visited every event in much detail, from her late husband's cellar accident, to the mist that spewed down the bedroom chimneys. At one stage, he asked her if she had ever practised witchcraft, which she found most infuriating. Reginald Spearing had to constantly remind the Inspector that he was unnecessarily revisiting facts from the previous interview. DI Dankworth's tack was that Mrs Baines might remember something that had not been mentioned previously.

The lengthy interview had become arduous and strenuous, when DI Dankworth raised his voice once more and spoke out to Annie,

'So, tell us Mrs Baines, why did you kill Detective Inspector Rita Judd?' That enraged Annie to raise her voice in return,

'I did not kill Inspector Judd, but I know who did.' There was a short pause, 'It was you that killed her Inspector. You pushed her in the grave and dropped the rock on her head. You had the motive to step into her shoes; step into this local-police department; move into the countryside away from Manchester. That rock was far too heavy for me to lift. You managed to lift it though; it was you that killed the Inspector, as yours' were the only fingerprints on the rock.'

'That's preposterous,' he retaliated, 'I removed the rock from her head to see if she was still alive.' DI Dankworth became agitated and terminated the interview.

CHAPTER 31 – THE CLOSURE

Annie spent the night in a police cell; she hated it. Detective Chief Superintendent Thackeray had called in a police psychiatrist to listen to parts of the interview recording with Detective Inspector Dankworth. Doctor Jenson Cartwright asked to speak directly to Annie afterwards. Detective Constable Liz Brentwood visited Annie's cell and explained the procedure. Annie would have to stay locked up in her cell all morning. She cussed; there was no chance for her to perform her cellar work at the start of the week, as she normally would, at this rate, she thought. Although the pub was closed, so it was not selling any beers, Annie compromised with herself.

Dr Cartwright listened to the recordings, made a few notes, not many, then proceeded to interview Annie. His first question was,

'Do you believe in the supernatural Mrs Baines?'

'Yes, I do,' she replied.

'Do you think there is a presence at Ye Olde Elm Tree?' the Doctor asked.

'Most definitely, multiple numbers of spirits,' replied Annie.

'Do you believe some of those spirits are vexed, angry?' he asked.

'Yes, extremely angry,' said Annie, 'The Theo Dawkins incident, during the séance, speaks for itself. My china cabinet pulled to the ground with some force.'

The psychiatrist confirmed, 'Theo Dawkins was an alleged spirit from one of the historic graves.'

'Yes, that's correct,' answered Annie.

'How long have you believed in the paranormal, Mrs Baines?' questioned Dr Cartwright.

'Only since we moved into Ye Olde Elm Tree,' she replied, 'From the very first month. I had a local customer, Vince Compton, he offered to build me a website for a few beers. Every Tuesday, I would pour him a pint, he would tell me all about his weekend, then on his second pint, I would take him upstairs to the office. On the third Tuesday, I had left the radio on in the office; as we entered the room, the music got louder and louder. I had to run over to the radio and turn it down. Vince declined to stay upstairs on that occasion. Then there were several incidents after that. My dog Chester, scaled the wall as if something had walked through it. The kettle switching itself on. Names called out. Chanting. Footsteps. Doors slamming. I never did get my website finished. I am still referred to as Mrs X on it today! All those unexplainable events spooked poor Vince, he even stopped visiting our pub.'

'Thank you for that Mrs Baines, most enlightening. Detective Inspector Dankworth mentioned witchcraft; have you ever studied witchcraft Mrs Baines?' asked Dr Cartwright. There was a pause.

'No. I have no idea where the Inspector dreamt up that notion. Perhaps it was whilst staying at Ye Olde Elm Tree. I had no choice but to put the Inspector in the most haunted room in the inn, on the top floor. He probably rubbed shoulders with a few of the pub's ghosts!' the Licensee replied emphatically.

The psychiatrist looked inquisitively at Annie. That in fact was a lie. Six months before her husband Bert died tragically in the cellar, Annie bought a book on white witchcraft. On one Halloween, Annie organised a 'witches circle' in Ye Olde Elm Tree. Four chairs placed in a nine feet diameter circle. On each chair a different coloured candle. Yellow for AIR, placed in the East, red for FIRE placed in the South, blue for WATER placed in the West, and green for EARTH placed in the North. Annie used salt to draw the circles lines; Bert thought she was mad at the time. She displayed to her punters that evening how to enter the circle, with fresh drawn lines; how to leave and break the circle by cutting the energy with a knife. One customer, Violet Dickinson, shouted obscenities when in the centre of the circle, toward her ex-husband, who was often violent toward her. Annie often pondered on that night. That poor gentleman was dead within a week.

Dr Jenson Cartwright asked Annie several more questions, but much to Annie's amazement there was not one question on the accidents, the murder, or missing persons at Ye Olde Elm Tree. His final question was,

'How could you possibly cope, Mrs Baines, with the unearthing of the vehicle and the three salesmen recovered, the other day. It must have brought back some unspeakable memories for you?' There was a long pause.

'I could not cope any longer Doctor. I immediately instructed a local property agency to put Ye Olde Elm Tree up for sale. I have had absolutely enough of the old place.' answered Annie, looking very sorrowful.

'Mrs Baines, I would recommend you conduct an exorcism at Ye Olde Elm Tree; it might just get rid of the odd unwanted psyche,' suggested Dr Cartwright. He smiled at Annie and thanked her for her honesty, shook her hand and left. He returned to DCS Thackeray's office.

'I am sorry Raj but you are going to have to let the poor woman go; you do not have enough evidence for a conviction. You do need to continue, however, with the excavations. Those graves are likely to contain your biggest clues in solving some of the mysteries around Ye Olde Elm Tree.'

The Superintendent looked perplexed. 'I am not sure how much longer we can subsidise the excavations, Jenson. We may have to find another way to fund them,' contemplated DCS Thackeray. Annie was released at 3.30 pm.

Annie returned to Ye Olde Elm Tree, she gave Chester the biggest hug, and made herself a strong cup of tea. She telephoned Rev Christopher Sallow; would he conduct an exorcism at Ye Olde Elm Tree? She almost begged him. He promised to telephone his bishop straight away.

The exorcism was all set for the Thursday morning. The reverend and his bishop were both in attendance. They would enter every room of Ye Olde Elm Tree with holy water and prayers.

'You must open all of the windows and all of the doors wide, throughout the inn, Mrs Baines,' requested Rev Sallow.

'Why?' asked Annie.

'The spirits need somewhere to escape,' was his reply. 'They need to be able to reach their astral realm. They need no restrictions, no containment; they must be free to pass on to the Elysian Fields beyond.' Annie obliged, walking ahead of them. She could not help but notice the old photograph of the King's Arms had fallen to the ground once more. They conducted the exorcism throughout the building. When they sanctified the snug, with holy water and prayers, they experienced a vibration; the floor shook, the new crockery in the china cabinet rattled. They all looked at each other with dread, but they carried on. At Annie's request, they continued to exorcise the shed and throughout the lower garden, where the historic graves had been exposed. Dr Bell, Dr Donnelly, and George Pullman watched on in slight trepidation.

DCS Raj Thackeray had arranged a meeting with Mr Fitzroy Ebanks, Head of Planning & Development at the County Council. The meeting was to discuss the ongoing excavations at Ye Olde Elm Tree. The police department was finding it difficult to continue to fund the anthropologist and archaeologist's work. Fortunately for the Superintendent, Mr Ebanks was able to assist. The County Council was underspent on their performing arts budget; some funding could be offered this way. In addition, the County Council were to receive a substantial grant from the Arts Council UK, to invest in arts and culture in the local area. Mr Ebanks also informed the Superintendent that he was about to write to the pub company concerning change of ownership of Ye Olde Elm Tree.

The weekend came with guests checking into Ye Olde Elm Tree as planned. Mr and Mrs King had travelled from South London. Mr Gough and Mr McSorley had travelled from Dublin. Annie prayed for a noneventful spiritual presence that weekend. There were no unwanted incidents, Annie wondered if the exorcism had been a success.

It was Detective Inspector Rita Judd's funeral. Annie wanted to pay her respects, despite being arrested and interrogated by the detective, she appreciated the Inspector was just trying to do her job. In contrast, she certainly would not have attended any funeral, had it been Detective Inspector Dankworth; she disliked him immensely. Annie persuaded Mollie to go with her. They stood at the back of the church and stood a long way from the graveside afterwards. DI Dankworth and DCS Thackeray were both annoyed that Annie Baines had attended the funeral of their respected officer. The next day, DI Dankworth would return to the Greater Manchester Police Department. Overall, he was disappointed with his achievements; the unearthing of the Mercedes and the three salesmen was his only real accomplishment. Detective Sergeant Roach had also spotted Annie Baines in the distance, and thought she had quite a nerve to attend the funeral. For DS Roach and DC Liz Brentwood, their eyes were fixed on Annie for long periods. There was a dark figure of a man, like a shadow, stood behind her; the silhouette's head was as if it was resting on Annie's shoulder. It was faceless. When Annie Baines and Mollie turned and started to walk back to the car, the figure followed them.

Over the following weeks, Dr Bell, Dr Donnelly, and George Pullman carried on the work of exposing further graves. Historian, Claudette Quail, was also under contract with the County Council. She was making considerable progress with ancestry tracing. At some point in the mid 1860's, Beacon House, on Beacon Hill, as it was called then, had changed ownership. From 1821 to 1861 censuses it was the residential property of the Gustav family. Earlier research found that the property was listed as Beacon Hill Farm. In the 1871 census the owners were Bart Livingstone, American, born in Marion, Indiana USA, aged twenty-five, married, profession; carpenter / preacher, living with his wife Arizona, born Bloomington, Indiana USA, same age, profession; dressmaker. In the 1881 census, two sons were recorded; Clayton, five and Virgil, four. Bart's profession remained carpenter / preacher. Arizona's profession had changed to pastor. In 1891 the same four were listed at Beacon House but Bart's profession was solely preacher. In 1901 the listing had changed. Bart and his youngest son Virgil were not listed. Arizona remained at Beacon House, as did her eldest son Clayton who had taken a wife, Queenie. They had two sons; William, four, James, three. Clayton Livingstone's profession was listed as a priest. Following in his father's footsteps, thought Claudette Quail. In the 1911 census, Clayton's family were listed at Beacon House, but Arizona was not listed.

It was then that Claudette studied records from the Great War. Sons, William and James, were recruited into the Border Regiment, a line infantry of the British Army. Clayton Livingstone was also detailed as a chaplain's assistant in the same regiment. All three men were lost in service, in 1916, in France, at the battle in Thiepval Woods. Claudette could not find any trace of Clayton's wife, Queenie. It was believed that Beacon House lay derelict for many years, until 1929 when a local builder, John Covington purchased the house together with accompanying farmland and religious site. Claudette believed the latter was a graveyard.

Claudette discovered the sale of farmland by John Covington to EGW Warren, an ancestor to local farmer Granville. She found a death record for John Covington in 1935. The same year, local brewer Benjamin Hoskins bought Beacon House at a local auction. There was no mention of religious land in the sale. Mr Hoskins was responsible for the property's change of use from residential to public house; the King's Arms. Her belief was that John Covington had buried over the entire graveyard to form a garden to the property, as it sloped downhill toward the neighbouring farmland and old elm tree.

Claudette had some further success with the Mormon Baptisms and Burials records. She discovered twenty-one baptisms and twenty-six burials, at the Wesleyan Chapel, Beacon Hill. This information was relayed to anthropologist Dr Cynthia Bell. The records ranged from 1868 to 1914, stopping at the outbreak of the First World War. Bart Livingstone was a Wesleyan Methodist preacher; a religious movement that promoted sinless life and anti-slavery. He practised from his residential home, yet referred to the premises as a chapel, without seeking formal change of use. Claudette Quail thought it ironic, that a movement that disapproved in the chapel, of the sale of tobacco and alcoholic beverages, forbidding secret societies, years on, became a public house.

Annie had a less eventful summer. The excavations continued. More graves were uncovered, the bodies originally exhumed were laid to rest once more. Guests came and went without having to experience a supernatural presence; much to Annie's relief. Objects moved or were knocked over in places, footsteps on freshly dug soil, even a small sink hole appeared in the car park. Annie exchanged contacts on the lease at the end of September, coinciding with the latter end of the tourist season. Fraser and Melanie Winterbottom also exchanged on their bed and breakfast business at the same time. Annie moved to Dorset to live with her sister Nancy.

Fitzroy Ebanks had written to the pub company, proposing a change of ownership, and submitting a compulsory purchase. The letter ended up on Director Douglas Winterbottom's desk. Douglas telephoned the company solicitor to seek advice.

'You should file it in File 13,' came the response. He had to explain to Douglas that File 13 is a euphemism for trash can, used by the US Military. Douglas chose to ignore the letter and filed it in the bottom drawer of his desk.

In the summer months, Ye Olde Elm Tree dart player Terry Thornley had approached local historian Claudette Quail. He was particularly interested in his great, great, great grandfather Aldrich Thornley, who shot his wife Eleanor and her lover, and had them buried together in the grounds of Ye Olde Elm Tree. Claudette identified Oswald Landry, buried on the same day as Eleanor at the Wesleyan Chapel. Aldrich, who was imprisoned for their murder, Claudette confirmed, died in the 1920's, so was not buried at Ye Olde Elm Tree. In the 1901 census at Heppleton Manor, Aldrich's profession was listed as a gun maker / journeyman. Claudette's interpretation of that was that he manufactured guns and sold them as a travelling salesman. For a short period, Terry would call in to Ye Olde Elm Tree for his usual pint and ask Annie if he could lay flowers on Eleanor's grave.

Annie's best friend, Chester, did not settle well at Nancy's house. The upheaval, the strange surroundings, Chester's condition deteriorated quite quickly. Annie's new chapter in her life would have to be without her soul companion.

Reporter Nick Fitzsimons continued to have nightmares about the bird attack he had experienced at Ye Olde Elm Tree. He would some nights wake up sweating profusely, his bed linen soaking. He sought psychiatric help once a week at a nearby lunatic asylum.

Ruben Hagen, injured by a dart at Ye Old Elm Tree, never fully recovered his sight in one eye. He worked in production at an electronics factory, but his partial sight impaired his vision somewhat, so he left his job to work on a farm. He never threw another dart.

The excavations continued for the best part of a year. Dr Bell and Dr Donnelly concluded the work once they had located the twenty-sixth grave. There was an eerie calm over the burial site. Photographer Gordon McLarty's body was recovered in the process, some twenty feet from the original dig. His ex-wife, Moira, was approached to see if she preferred Gordon's remembrance to be in Glasgow where she lived. She was not comfortable with the proposal, so Gordon was buried at Ye Olde Elm Tree site, a twenty-seventh grave. Only Reverent Sallow, Nick Fitzsimons and a newspaper editor attended the burial.

The wrangle over change of ownership continued for a further two years. The dispute reached the high court eventually, but it was granted in favour of the County Council. Douglas Winterbottom fought for compensation for his nephew Fraser and his wife Melanie. Once he achieved this, the company asked Douglas to step down as director. Fraser and Melanie invested their hard-earned compensation in a ten-bedroom hotel. The hotel was within walking distance of the beach. Fraser would often go down there with his metal detector, found one day in Ye Olde Elm Tree car park, no one had ever claimed it.

The County Council Arts and Culture group had the responsibility of deciding what to do with Ye Olde Elm Tree. They decided to turn it into a museum, representing the previous uses of the property. There would be a section on local farming, mainly of the early 19th century. There would be a section on when it was habited as a Wesleyan Chapel. There would be two wall plaques; one listing registered baptisms with names and dates, another for burials. The graveyard would be fully restored. Claudette Quail was contracted onto the team at the beginning of the project. The third section was dedicated to a public house and inn. There would be dedications to when it was called the King's Arms, and in later years Ye Olde Elm Tree. The pub sign outside would remain. A large sign 'Museum' was fixed to the front wall; some thought, this was to discourage passers-by stopping off for a drink. The main bar was the obvious choice for the public house section. The cellar would be kept as authentic as possible. The snug would be converted into a chapel; there would be funds available to have an altar made. The upstairs, with a few doorways introduced to link rooms together, would be converted into a local historic farming section. The two rooms on the top floor were to be used for office and storage. There were plans to build a covered lean-to on the back of the kitchen. The intention being to accommodate a café, in the warmer tourist seasons.

The following spring, neighbouring farmer Granville stopped his tractor near the museum garden fence and admired the way in which the council had re-established the Wesleyan graveyard. Headstones and graves preserved, new grave markers, uniformed grass verges and beds of brightly coloured artificial flowers. He looked at the old elm tree at the bottom of the garden. He noticed there were no buds on it at all; it had started to die.

Annie and Nancy had booked bargain interconnecting flights to New Zealand. From London there would be a four hour stop-over in Dubai, before flying on to Auckland.

'What are we going to do for four hours in Dubai International airport?' asked Nancy.

'Shopping,' yelled Annie quite excitedly.

The two ladies had different shopping styles. Annie was a clothes shopper; she always tried to look presentable when working in Ye Olde Elm Tree. Nancy was one to look around the jewellery and perfume shops. When they were safely inside the airport complex, they decided to split up for an hour to shop separately, then meet up under the large digital clock, have something to eat, washed down with a few glasses of wine. Time soon passed and the two ladies were soon boarding the aircraft again for their final journey. Forty minutes into the flight, Dubai Air Traffic Control lost radar contact with flight MKM 6144. The flight did not reach the destination of Auckland. Edgar Baines travelled to the airport to meet Annie and Nancy. His journey was in vain.

Barry Hillier